Tammy Norrie

William Hershaw is a poet, musician and songwriter. He is Principal Teacher of English at Beath High School, Cowdenbeath. His works in Scots and English include *Fower Brigs Tae A Kinrik* published by Aberdeen University Press and *The Cowdenbeath Man* published by the Scottish Cultural Press. He has also written two textbooks on the teaching of Scots Language in the Secondary school published by Learning Teaching Scotland. He wrote *A Mass In Scots For Saint Andrae's Day*.

In 2005 he won the Callum MacDonald Memorial Award for Poetry and in 2011 he was awarded the McCash Prize for Scots Poetry by Glasgow University. In 2007 he collaborated with sculptor David Annand, writing the poem *God The Miner* which is inscribed on the statue *The Prop* as part of the Lochgelly Regeneration Project.

Recently he has co - edited the Literary Magazine *Fras* along with Walter Perrie and has published *HappyLand,* a selection of new poems with an accompanying CD of readings and music. In November 2012 *Cage Load Of Men - The Joe Corrie Project* by The Bowhill Players was released. Funded by Fife Council, Willie Hershaw has written the musical settings for the poems of the legendary Fife poet and playwright. *Tammy Norrie* is his first novel.

Tammy Norrie

The Hoose Daemon Of Seahouses

William Hershaw

GRACE NOTE PUBLICATIONS
OCHTERTYRE

Tammy Norrie:The Hoose Daemon Of Seahouses
first published in 2013
by GRACE NOTE PUBLICATIONS C.I.C.

GRACE NOTE PUBLICATIONS
Grange of Locherlour,
Ochtertyre, PH7 4JS,
Scotland

books@gracenotereading.co.uk
www.gracenotepublications.co.uk

ISBN 978-1-907676-43-7

A catalogue record for this book is available
from the British Library

Cover photographs: Margaret Bennett

Typeset by Grace Notes, Ochtertyre

For Andrew and David

Hae ye seen ma laddie?
Na, he disnae ging tae schuil.
Nae langer deaved by hours and rooms,
he guddles in the puils.

Ablaw the lichthoose Venus
he's there wi net and jaur,
he's sib wi cells that pulse wi virr,
as unthirlt as the scaurs.

Gin ye see ma laddie
in the gloamin on his lane
juist tell him that I lou him,
and that suin I'll caa him hame.

CHAPTER ONE

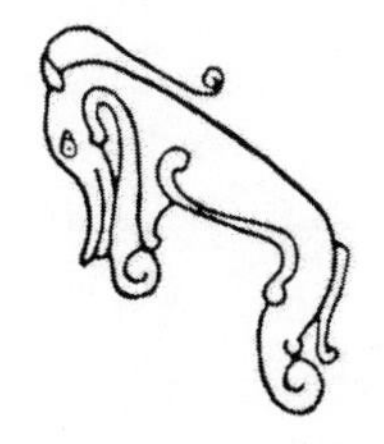

Oh No, Not Again

Dance to your Daddy, my little laddy
Dance to your Daddy, my little man
Thou shalt have a fish and thou shalt have a fin
Thou shalt have a codlin when the boat comes in
Thou shalt have haddock baked in a pan
Dance to your Daddy, my little man

Dance to your Daddy, my little laddie
Dance to your Daddy, my little man
When thou art a young boy, you must sing and play
Go along the shore and cast your shells away
Build yourself a castle, watch the tide roll in
Dance to your Daddy, my little man.

Dance to your Daddy, my little laddie
Dance to your Daddy, my little man
When thou art a young man, go unto the trades
Find yourself a skill, and wages you'll be paid
Then with all your wages, buy yourself some land
Dance to your Daddy, my little man

Dance to your Daddy, my little laddie
Dance to your Daddy, my little man
When thou art a man and go to take a wife
Find yourself a lass and love her all your life
She shall be your wife and thou shalt be her man
Dance to your Daddy, my little man

Dance to your Daddy, my little laddie
Dance to your Daddy, my little man
When thou art an old man, father to a son
Sing to him the old songs, sing of all you've done
Pass along the old ways, then let his song begin
Dance to your Daddy, my little man

Ugh! Aargh! They've arrived. I hear them before I see them. What do I hear? I hear the squish and skirl of a large ugly four wheel drive bullying and pushing its way through our narrow entrance close, going far too fast. Then the awful thing brakes hard on the prepared neatly raked gravel forecourt, making my old bowels shrivel and clench. It's the Blackberries, a well off family of four pests, come to share my house and give me no peace. I'll have to put up with them through all of Easter week. Of course, I'll do my level best to make sure their holiday turns out as unpleasant and uncomfortable as possible – but there's only so much that a single wee hoose daemon can do. They'll never see me or notice anything amiss no matter how roundly I curse them – folk like the Blackberries never notice anything but their own needs and wants.

My name is Tammy Norrie – I am a hoose daemon, spirit, invisible ghost – eel, animus – whatever you choose to call me. I bide in and haunt an old fisherman's cottage called *Jonah's Neuk* at Seahouses on the cold windy coast of Northumberland. Sadly, the generations of fisher folk who lived in former days in *Jonah's Neuk* have all set sail for *Fiddler's Green* now. Belle, Willie The Scotsman, Old Hilda, Young Bert, Young Hilda, Doris. Only me left here. Me and Nicey. The house was sold eighteen months ago after Young Hilda passed away at the age of one hundred and seven and converted into a holiday home for tourists who come to the North East. But not as regularly as the new owner, Farquhair Tinkerson, hoped when he had the house renovated for his modern holiday clients. Apparently there is yet another economic recession going on in the wide world beyond Seahouses and many folk can hardly afford to get by from week to week let alone come to the seaside for a holiday. So it seems, that for the time being at least, Farquhair has wasted his precious money. For months at a time, especially in deep winter when the winds sing and birl around the chimney pots, *Jonah's Neuk* lies empty and I have the house and its history and memories all to myself. I suppose that is why I resent the intrusion bitterly when visitors do come. I know that sounds cranky and cantankerous and ungracious but perhaps if I tell you a bit about my life you will understand.

Seahouses is a little coastal town that huddles itself around its harbour and faces out to the tumbling grey North Sea and the low rocky Farne Islands – famous for puffins, seals, lighthouses and the heroine Grace Darling who old Bob Cod once met. It can be very busy on Sunday afternoons, bank holidays and sometimes for a few weeks in summer if there is a spell of good weather and a patch of bright blue sky. Then the smell of frying fat and fish and chips and vinegar wafts everywhere from the white vans and stalls that cluster round the harbour. Crab nets on bamboo sticks, beach balls and spades, buckets and gaudy coloured plastic kites spill out of shop fronts on to the crowded pavements. People arrive in their cars and book boat trips to sail out to the Farnes. Old folk daunder about, leaning on their sticks and frames. They remember things then have a nice sit down on benches while the bored bairns greet and whine until they are given ice cream and cans of juice to stop their noise. It is on days like these that the ancient pubs are packed full of chattering folk who have travelled up from Newcastle for the day or down from the Scottish Borders or driven from even further away. But it is not always like this and it was not always like this either. Even on the hottest of days a draught springs up from somewhere to remind us that where we are is usually a cold place and that beside us rolls the cold and untamable North Sea.

On breezy summer nights I like to roost up on the rattling pantiles of my house next to the birling chimney granny. From up there I can look North to the cranellated ramparts of Bamburgh Castle. Beyond lies the cone shaped tower of Lindisfarne and sometimes, dim and shimmery in the distance, I can make out far Saint Abb's Head. Somewhere behind Saint Abb's I know the great river Forth pours out of East Scotland into the North Sea. I would like to go there someday. I would love to visit Edinburgh and see the castle. Mostly though, I gaze out to the East, especially when it is growing dark and the lengthy beam from Longstone lighthouse is beginning to stretch its ghostly arm out across the grey North Sea. I think back over fifteen decades to when I was a wee bairn daemon . . . Seahouses was still a fishing village then and its inhabitants were all fisher folk. Occasionally, a handful of well off Victorian visitors would turn up to stay at the Inns, latterly, having arrived on the newly opened North Sunderland line, having disembarked at the Station where the car park now stands. They would come here to visit the Farnes, having heard about *wor Gracie*, birdwatch or to take in the healthy bracing air and pace up and down the beach, the men in their long coats and tall hats, talking seriously with their hands behind their straightened backs. The women wore long skirts and big floppy hats that would always blow off in the wind unless they were tied under their chin by silk ribbons. The Victorians were ones for their daft hats . . . but that was long ago, although not as long ago as some of Bob Cod's stories . . .

The Blackberries are unpacking. They are noisy and fractious. I am watching them from the upstairs window. They cannot see me and they would never think to lift their heads away from themselves and their affairs anyway. None of them seem to like each other or be able to get on and co-operate with each other in any way. The husband and his wife are arguing about who was responsible for bringing what. "You won't need it anyway," insists Mr. Blackberry. They seem to have brought plenty stuff with them. Then Mr. Blackberry's phone makes its annoying ringtone. It's meant to be funny. It's an Irish comedian shouting "Answer the fecking phone!" It's not funny. It's someone from his office. He turns his back on his family and starts to talk into his shiny new phone. Mrs. Blackberry is not happy at having to unpack the car on her own and grumbles at her husband as she carries the holdalls and rucksacks and dumps them down in the hall. "I'll take them this far but you have to unpack them,Mark!" she barks at her husband who is ignoring her, busy with his business conversation. The two boys are supposed to be helping but become bored with helping quickly. In fact, they never start. The older boy sits on a rucksack and starts to read a book about a wizard killing goblins. The younger one demands his football from the car boot. "It's at the back, I'll get it just now , if you can wait a minute." sighs Mrs Blackberry distractedly.

"But I need it now!" whines the younger boy. "I'm bored with being in this car!"

The older brother looks up from his book and scoffs at the younger. "I'm *bored* with being in the car" he mimics in an exaggerated whiney baby voice, "you're not actually *in* the car, stupid baby . . . Ouch! Mum – he just slapped me! That was sore you little creep. He slapped me on the head, Mum! Do something!

Look!" The older brother tries to hit his younger brother on the head with his book in retaliation but misses as the younger boy quickly ducks and runs away laughing. The goblin book flies from his hand on to the gravel. "Look what you made me do, you annoying little toad."

"Ha, ha!"

"Would you two shut up right now before I ground you both," bawls father Blackberry.

"Stop shouting at them!" shouts his wife.

"Sorry Jack," says Mr Blackberry on the phone, "I wasn't shouting at you . . ."

"I want to play football," says the younger brother, "and I need my football boots. Mum – I need my football boots."

"Your Dad will play football with you," says Mrs Blackberry, " I'm tired from the car journey. I need a rest."

The youngest Blackberry is not happy. No one is paying him any attention and he needs constant attention of any kind, all of the time. He begins to kick up the gravel, digging his toe and making a hole in the smooth gravel forecourt. He is kicking up a little cloud of dust. From the window I watch him slyly turning the point of his attack around until he is kicking dust and little chips of gravel in the direction of his older brother. Furtively, he looks up and laughs. But his father catches him. "Ronnie! Stop it now! I've warned you already . . ."

Ronald stops at once and turns around away from his father in a put on huff. But he doesn't stop kicking gravel. Now he is kicking chips of gravel on to the wall of *Jonah's Neuk*, pinging the window panes. Mrs. Blackberry has gone into the house and is reading her Kindle, drinking a glass of wine and phoning her friends to complain about the quality of the local primary school where they live. "Both of you, in the house – now! Ronnie – I'm not paying for a new window pane. If you break that it's coming out of your holiday money." roars Mr. Blackberry. "Sorry Jack – no, that wasn't aimed at you . . . yes, I can make a week on

Tuesday."

And so it goes and so it will be for a long, long week until they pack up and leave and I am left in blessed peace. Occasionally they will venture out, after much rowing and complaining, on a trip somewhere, coming back more fractious than when they left, having disturbed everyone they encounter. They're constant. But at least then I will get some respite. But when all four of the perfect pests are in my house it is horrible. It is constant shouting and screaming and crying and banging and rows and complaints and huffs and accusations. There is little to be done but to endure it. So I make myself as small as I can and head for a favourite sanctuary. Through the small crack at the back of the lid I slither into the cistern of the toilet. I take a deep breath and dive into the cold tank under the water, wrapping my snake like body around the ballcock. In here it is dark and much of the noise outside is diffused – angry voices become faint gurgles and hopefully I can snatch some sleep for an hour or so. That is until little Ronnie, who is bored, comes in and flushes the toilet. Then flushes it – again and again and again. Welcome Blackberries – have a lovely holiday.

CHAPTER TWO

A Walk In The Sea

During the night I do my best to make them think the house is haunted – which it is, in a way, because I'm here. I've had some limited success with this in the past. Alas! No joy. Ronald and Reginald take a while to get to sleep. They are up pillow fighting, arguing about which bed, being sick, being too hot, being too cold and needing drinks until well after midnight. By one o'clock both are out like snuffed candles, worn out by a day of annoying each other and everyone else they have inflicted themselves upon. Mr. Blackberry is not the type to be scared by phantom thoughts and suggestions – he does not possess the imagination required for that and is soon snoring loudly, no doubt dreaming of the deals he will make on his phone in the morning with John, Jimmy and Jack. Mrs. Blackberry, who is a fretful, highly strung woman, is my best bet. She lies abed, reading her Kindle until late on, but soon she too nods off, tired by her car journey and constantly placating her two pests. I limber up by trying a few moves for later on in the week: making doors and joists creak suddenly, whistling along water pipes and – a tough ask – trying to flick the kitchen light switch back on. Slamming doors I don't have the strength for these days. A half full wine glass has been left on the coffee table. I rush and charge and try to push it over the table edge but again, these days I don't have the kind of oomph I used to. I can't raise the wind to blow it over. It's a pity because a glass smashing by itself in the middle of the night can be quite dramatic and sow a wee seed of doubt in a jittery mind. Being upset by the Blackberries and having your routine changed can be tiring in its own way and after a while I head up to the attic space to cuddle in with my pal Nicey.

I'm up very early though and head on down to the beach for a tear about in the wind. I love it down there at this time when there's no one around on the greying beach and I can splash about dancing a jig to the silver music of the tide. Whahey Man! I shake the salty water out of my gills and bounce along the sand in the breeze to dry myself. Back up the street and still damp, I smell the pungent aroma from the Old Fish Smokery. It's opened early. I shin up the drainpipe on to the roof and curl myself round the hot smokey chimney to get a heat in me. No need to go back in the noisy house just yet. The Blackberries will be getting up in grumpy moods, complaining about not having a decent power shower or Sky TV.

It's not that I don't like bairns. I was one myself once – though not like little Ronald and Reginald. Bairns are like grown ups – you get good ones, bad ones and all sorts in between. But these days I see more bad ones and the main reason for it, as far as I can see, is that their parents are too useless or selfish or stupid to give them a good kick up the backside or whatever it is that they need or deserve to stop being so badly behaved. I shudder to think what some of these kids will turn into but I suppose that's not my worry. The problem is, their daft parents don't think it's their worry either. But who am I to talk? – I didn't ever have parents. But enough about me . . .

. . . I'll tell you about the three women who lived in *Jonah's Neuk* in my time. All who lived full and eventful lives.

There were three generations of women who lived in *Jonah's Neuk* in the time that I have lived here – Belle, Old Hilda and Young Hilda. They were all special but Young Hilda was my favourite for reasons I will tell you about later on. I remember them all more clearly than the men. In the old days, the women ruled the house. It was their domain. The men went out to sea to fish. It was a tough and dangerous job and in their little boats the risk of death from drowning was very great. Storms and rocks and even freak waves could come along and sweep them into the waters to meet the cold green angels at any time. The men could be away for days at the fishing. When they came home they would have a sleep then soon be away down to the harbour to mend nets, fix creels, repair tackle, paint the scarred underbellies of their boats or barter with the fish merchants. If they had no money, which was often, they might just be hanging around the quayside till teatime, blethering and boasting. If they had a penny or two they would be in the pub spending it on brown ale. It was only during bad weather with no money that they would be forced to stay in the house, sullen and fretful and getting scolded for being good for nothings by their wives and told to get their feet down. No, men didn't belong in the house. Bairns belonged there sometime – but not in summer. Women ruled the roost – always.

In the case of Belle, you couldn't blame her husband, poor Willie the Scotsman, for not wanting to come home some nights. It was well known that she battered him and that he was terrified of her. Many a cold night she locked the door on him and he had to sleep in the shed or in the hold of *The Glad Tidings*. Belle was a fearsome women. She was built like a fish barrel. Tiny but as broad as she was long and immensely strong with great red beefy arms on her and a boxer's pugnacious jaw. Because I was young in those days she always seemed older to me but when I first saw her she could barely have been out of her twenties. In those days folk grew up quicker. There were no such things as teenagers. You left school on the Friday aged thirteen or fourteen and the next Monday morning you were an adult earning a living. In looks and clothes and speech and manner you were grown up and expected to contribute. Belle had always been old, I suspect. She was as tough as an old sea boot. As a girl she had travelled up and down the East Coast from Yarmouth to Fraserburgh, gutting the shoals of herring that were so abundant in those days. It was hard work and the fisherlassies had to stand in the cold and the weather slitting open the bellies of the little silver purses with their flashing knives, their fingers red raw and bandaged, flipping away the fishy smelling pink insides before flinging them into barrels to be packed with coarse salt. They sang as they worked. Even in old age Belle was reckoned to be handy with a gulley knife and you didn't mess with her. In the summer, when there was a low tide and the boats had to be pulled up out of the stinking sucking putrid mud to be painted, Belle would come down and roll up her sleeves, outpulling the men as the boats were dragged up to the grass to be scraped before given their Sunday best. One Good Friday she got roaring drunk in *The Schooner.* The Skipper of *The Serendipity* happened to be in and, drunk himself, passed a comment about the treatment that Belle doled out to poor Willie the Scotsman which Belle over heard. The skipper ended up missing his four front teeth and had two thunderously black eyes when they carried him out on an unhinged door. The Landlord, from a safe distance behind the bar, cursed Belle as if he were the Prince Bishop of Durham Cathedral himself and swore that she would never be allowed to set foot in *The Schooner* again – and that she would pay for every bit of damage she had caused – which was plenty.

The next Friday, Belle calmly walked back into *The Schooner* as if nothing had happened and asked for her usual large tumbler of rum and sugar. The landlord said, "Now Belle – I hope you are going to behave yourself today and that there will be no repetition of the disgraceful behaviour of last weekend. . ." Belle just laughed at him and spat her brown chewing tobacco onto the flagged floor. But she behaved herself and no more was said or done. Certainly nobody ever commented on her treatment of poor Willie the Scotsman ever again . . .

When I get back to the house little Ronnie is running amok. The Blackberries have been out for a walk around the town but Ronnie has soon gotten bored and demanded that he be bought the first thing he sees – in this case a plastic Viking helmet with horns and war axe accessory. Bob Cod once told me that the real Vikings didn't have horns on their helmets and that this was a modern invention. Unaware of this or even that he is wearing a Viking helmet Ronnie has, nevertheless, picked up on the general idea of what that violent Northern race were all about. He is running around the house berserk and screaming lustily while whacking the furniture good style with his war axe. He scythes the tops from some artificial bull rushes that have been placed in a tall vase. He has a quick look around to see if he has been spotted. No one has, so he stuffs the tops down the vase and careers merrily on his way, screaming and bawling beastily in bloodlust. As is often the case with little Ronnie, the screaming suddenly ceases. There is an awful second or two of pregnant silence when it seems like the whole house is drawing in its breath in preparation for what comes next – then an ear piercing scream emits followed by a soul wrenching wail that would wake all the dead sailors of Seahouses.

"Mam, mam!" Ronnie comes running through, tears streaming down his contorted face. "I've hurt my fingers!" he sobs. And he has. They're black and blue. "Ha! Ha! Serves you right." laughs Reginald. Having decided to take an extra vicious whack at the bookcase, his plastic axe blade has buckled and Ronnie has staved his fingers on the wooden bookcase. The bookcase is a solid object. One of the few possessions of Young Hilda that were not carted off to the auction house when *Jonah's Neuk* was emptied and replaced with cheap Ikea tourist furniture. The bookcase has hit back against the Vikings. Ronnie will be in hysterics for a long time and demand much in way of compensation.

Bob Cod, before he left for *Fiddlers' Green*, claimed he had lived in houses around here for over twelve hundred years. Certainly, in the past, there were plenty of house daemons living around Seahouses and, like characters in the Old Testament, they all seemed to live for a very long time. Now the old fishermens' homes have all been converted into holiday apartments and the house daemons are all long gone except for me. I was the youngest of them and now I'm the last. There used to be Bob, myself, Lang Lamphray, Sandy Eilden, Harry Haddock the mathematician, Wullie Whitebait, Wee Lingy, Scampy Finnan, Roller Skate, Crabby Pincer, Bedey Monkfish and Seabasstian Haik. On still summer nights we would roost on our roof trees and hold a blethers' parliament, shouting and hooting abuse at each other astride our chimney stacks.

Bob Cod claimed he could mind the coming of the Vikings to Lindisfarne and the burning of the priory and the routing of the poor old baldy monks. He was a terrible liar, though maybe he was telling the truth on this occasion. You could never tell with Bob. Some of what he said had a grain of truth in it that had been polished by Bob's imagination until it grew into a lustrous pearl of a yarn. Bob said that when the wonderful illuminated Lindisfarne gospels had tumbled toward the foaming fingers of brine in the boat of the frantic fleeing brothers he had caught the book and held it just above the churning whale's acre of wet waves until a brother bent and hauled the thing back unspoiled. They had considered this a great miracle that the precious book was recovered undamaged by the damp fingers of the salty sea and they had prayed in their boat on their knees to their Christian

God (who annoyed and upset the Vikings intensely) for this miracle and sign that they would all be saved. When I questioned him closely, Bob could not explain clearly what he was doing, swimming in the sea like a fat dolphin in his trunks at that time alongside the monk's boat. He said he had gone up to Lindisfarne to fly his kite, up there among the tall dunes.

"By Saint Cuthbert's beads!" exclaimed Wullie Whitebait, when Bob had finished. However Roller Skate, the bespectacled daemon of the local doctor's house, which contained a small but comprehensive library, later confirmed to me that all this might be true. For some reason, Roller Skate was always inclined to give Bob the benefit of the doubt, perhaps because he admired his creativity and enjoyed hearing his stories. Bob said it had been a fine sunny breezy day in June with the incoming tide sparkling like jewels. He told it well. The meek mannered monks, all men of God, going about their well ordered day: some praying in their cells, some writing and illuminating, some tending the beehives, some brewing ale, some picking healing herbs like rue and sorrel from the garden for the sick pilgrims who came across the causeway every day. Then someone had seen something. A red speck on the horizon. The sail of an unknown boat, sailing in from the North East. What kind of boat might it be with a red sail like that? Uneasiness grew to apprehension, which turned into fear which turned into panic as an imperious dragon prow became visible and finally coarse and guttural threats were heard ringing from afar and the frantic beating of swords on thick wooden shields. Then it was grab what you can and get into a boat and away fast. They left the dregs of the altar wine in the chalice for the Vikings to fight over, the bannocks burning in the clay oven, matins unsaid.

As Roller Skate was the best read among us it was to him we often turned with questions that concerned us about who and what we were and why we are here. These are all important questions but on the other hand I sometimes think they have no importance at all – we all have a selfish view of things. "The Gull's God is never a fish" as Lingy always said. We're here because we're here so best to get on with it. This is what Roller Skate told me about the Viking raid on Lindisfarne in his dry, scholarly, smoker's coughing fashion.

"Ahem. Well now, young Sandy – in 793 AD, a Viking raid on Lindisfarne caused much consternation throughout the Christian west, and is now often taken as the beginning of the Viking Age. It says in the Anglo Saxon Chronicle and I quote, ahem :

"In this year fierce, foreboding omens came over the land of Northumbria. There were excessive whirlwinds, lightning storms, and fiery dragons were seen flying in the sky (this would be Bob Cod's kite, no doubt). These signs were followed by great famine, and on the eighth of January the ravaging of heathen men destroyed God's church at Lindisfarne."

The more popularly accepted date for the Viking raid on Lindisfarne is 8th June; the editor of Routledge's edition of the Anglo-Saxon Chronicle, writes "*vi id Ianr*, presumably is an error for *vi id Iun* (June 8th) which is the date given by the *Annals of Lindisfarne* (p. 505), when better sailing weather would have favoured Viking coastal raids. Now isn't that interesting, young Sandy?Alcuin, a Northumbrian scholar in Charlemange's court at the time, said, and ahem, I quote again:

"Never before has such terror appeared in Britain as we have now suffered from a pagan race. . . .The heathens poured out the blood of saints around the altar, and trampled on the bodies of saints in the temple of God, like dung in the streets."

He doesn't seem too pleased about it. These Viking raids in 875 led to the monks fleeing the island with St Cuthbert's bones (The bones of St Cuthbert are now buried at the Cathedral in Durham, by the way, or maybe not). The bishopric was transferred to Durham in AD 1000. A fateful year. The Lindisfarne Gospels apparently now reside in the British Library in London, which is a bloody cheek – ahem, pardon my language – as they should reside back here in the North East where they rightfully belong. The priory was re-established in Norman times in 1093 as a Benedictine house and continued until its suppression in 1536 under Henry VIII. Ahem – that's all you need to know."

Thanks Roller Skate.

Now if you read all that and take it in, it would seem that Bob's story seems to be mixing up two historical dates – the first Viking raid in 793 and the one in 875. When I asked Bob about this he just shrugged and said something about his memory not being as reliable as it used to be. "Sorry kidda", he said. Roller Skate remarked wryly that Bob's memory was a good example of oral transmission and how the folk tradition operated but I don't know what he meant by that. Bob Cod also claims to have seen the artists William Turner and Charles Rennie MacIntosh painting at separate times when he was flying his kite on subsequent visits to the dunes of Holy Island.

Lingy, another hoose daemon, had a poor opinion of the Vikings. "They were the first capitalists, me bonny lads – make no mistake aboot that. They had nae natural resources or owt they were makkin themselves to speak of but they knew the value of everything – whether it be otter and beaver skins, jewels, coins, swords, ivory, slaves, bronze, silver or gold. They liked their material wealth, the Vikings did. And what they didn't have, they helped themselves to – just took it wi violence and murder and carried it aff hame like wi them. They knawed whit they were aboot the Vikings like. That's whit they were daein at Lindisfarne – the erse had faan oot the Bronze and Iron age markets like and they were lookin tae get their hands on some new gear. Mind you, they hated the Christians as weel and I diven't blame them for that. They've been nae freends tae us daemons either, the Christians. Aye, love thy neebour but burn the bloody hoose daemons – that's generally the story like."

Ronnie's Mum has now put cream on his sore fingers. He has stopped howling and is glaring balefully at the bookcase. The bookcase does not look bothered.

CHAPTER THREE

Run For Home

After much wailing and gnashing of teeth, the Blackberries are away out for the day on a trip to Bamburgh Castle, leaving me with the house all to myself and to remember things the way they used to be. They'll be home early and it will all end up in tears.

Belle lived well into the new century, fulfilling her wish "to see out the old Queen" by a good margin, a decade in fact, but she was also the shortest lived of the three mistresses of *Jonah's Neuk*. She had lived a hard life and it finally took its toll. She also outlived her husband, poor Willie the Scotsman, by almost twenty years and she remained physically active and mentally strong until her last few days, bossing and intimidating everyone she met. Despite her strong temper and volatility, in private she was an honest, hard working woman, though not always a sober one or a god fearing one (though I don't think she ever understood her own capacity to put the fear of God into others). She was completely without vanity and never looked in a mirror so she had no idea how fearsome she appeared with her crooked teeth and pugnacious mouth and haddocky face. She had nothing about her of what we now think of as ego and ambition. She accepted life as it was given to her and got on with it in her own way. She could barely read or write, having received little education. As a wee girl she had been forced to work to help provide for the family as in those days there was no call for a working class girl to receive any schooling at all, there being no prospects of a career or employment where any formal education would be necessary. On the days when the boats were due to sail to the fishing grounds the men would lie abed while the women folk were up from five o'clock baiting haddock lines with mussels – a smelly, messy and never ending job. It was crippling on the hands and fingers too. Miles of line had to be baited. Belle was tough. She could drink any man under the table. She never had a very high opinion of men in general (a view shared by her grand daughter) so she never remarried after poor Willie the Scotsman's death. In her last few years, when she spent more time in the house, she sometimes took down the tattered old family bible from the high fire place shelf besides the two china dogs and she would stumble over the strange words in that old book, trying to make some sense of the weird unforgiving stories of the Old Testament. Once a neighbour walked in unexpectedly (folk didn't lock their doors in those days) and came upon her trying to read the book of Revelations, following the words laboriously with her fingers and sounding them out. She behaved as guiltily as if she had been caught in the act of shop lifting.

One cold January morning Belle didn't get up at the crack of dawn as usual. She had died in the night in her sleep. She had left no will. After the funeral her only child and daughter Hilda, who later became known to all as Old Hilda, moved back into *Jonah's Neuk* with her husband, young Bert, who was a fisherman. Hilda, who was a lot quieter and had much of her father's desire for peace and a life without confrontation had been glad to escape from her mother's domineering influence when she married even though it meant that she and Bert had been living in a cramped attic room with Bert's parents, which was a common arrangement back then. Although there was no will to be had, it was seen by all as perfectly fair that Belle's only child inherited the house and the transition passed off smoothly without any greedy solicitors getting their hands on any money.

I often wondered about Belle's harsh treatment of poor Willie the Scotsman, because despite her faults she was not an ungenerous or wicked – hearted individual. Certainly, she could be daunting, she was generally on her mettle and people were wary of her. She could be "always on the face of a battle" as the saying goes. I think that was how she saw life – a kind of perpetual struggle and if you admitted to any weakness you might go under the waves. On the other hand, if a neighbour was in trouble she would be the first to chap on the door with an offer of help. She kept a tea caddy with coppers and thruppennies and if anyone was suffering financial hardship she would donate what she had with no expectation of repayment. She knitted shawls and clothes for new born bairns and she had plenty patience and a blether and the time of day for the old folk for whom she often made soup. Guisers at Halloween would be given treacle scones but the rest of the year the bairns avoided her and called her a *crubbit auld witch.* I imagine, with some relish, how young Ronnie would fare with Belle as his Granny for a day. I think Belle saved up all her frustrations and negative feelings about life and took it out on poor Willie – why? Because he was there and because he never fought back or challenged and because he seemed to accept Belle as someone who could not be changed – a force of nature. If you had asked Belle if she had enjoyed a happy life she would not have understood the question. She would have been puzzled first then that would have made her angry. Folk in her situation and class at that time did not think in these terms. Life was to be endured, survived – *tholed* to use a Scots word poor Willie often came out with. If an opportunity arose to have a laugh or a good time, sing a song or have a glass of beer then you had to grab it with both hands but there was no expectation that a laugh or a good time was a certainty or due to you. Tragedy could occur at any time – even on Christmas Day (usually a low key occasion back then and not the palaver it is today).

There was, perhaps, another reason for Belle's continual animosity toward poor Willie the Scotsman.Under the saggy old bed that Old Hilda inherited from Belle, lay, well hidden, a tin which contained a ring, letters and some newspaper cuttings. This might seem curious since Belle could hardly read. A clue lay in the date printed on the newspaper cuttings: October 15th, 1881. The day after Black Friday.

1881 had been a terrible year right up the East coast for all the fisherfolk. Storms in the spring had disrupted the haddock fishing and catches had been poor. Then in the summer in the Shetland Islands to the North, fifty men from a village called *The Gloup* on the island of Yell lost their lives when a terrible storm swept down from Iceland and drowned them all. As the back end of the year approached there was real hardship and poverty in the fishing communities and the men were all desperate to set sail to try to earn some money before Christmas from the thick and populous shoals of herring that congregated at that time in such abundance that as Bob Cod used to say "you could walk from boat to boat across the sea without getting your feet wet."

That Friday morning dawned calm and bright with the sea as calm as a mill pond.

But there was a heavy, eerie ominous feeling about the town. A feeling of unease and impending dread. However, when the fishermen of Eyemouth took a stroll down to the quayside, the barometer that was nailed on a post there read as low as they had ever seen it – the pressure was so low a mighty storm had to be on the way. Yet the young men did what young men always do when the old boys foretell doom and gloom. They just shrugged their shoulders. *We've been in stormy weather before and came home safely they said. We'll be out and back again before any storm. Besides, we all need the money. Debts have to be paid.*

One young man who was even keener than the rest to set sail was Thomas Fairbairn. He was betrothed to be married to an English Lassie from Seahouses that November. He had first met her eighteen months before in Yarmouth in a shoreside pub when his boat had put in there. She was working as a fish gutter. Thomas was young but ambitious. He wanted to skipper his own boat. Belle had told him there was a chance of him getting an old boat in Seahouses and doing it up. He had been saving up but he needed much more.

One good catch might swing it.

Meanwhile on the quayside there was much discussion. Honour dictated that if one boat set sail from Eyemouth then all must set sail. Eventually fifty fishing boats left on the flat calm sea past the Hurkar Rocks in close formation. An old man was overheard to say *Aye – but they'll no come hame that wey.* They arrived at the fishing grounds about eleven miles to the east of Eyemouth about eleven. Almost immediately the sky turned dark, what wind there was dropped completely and it grew so silent and still that there wasn't a sound to be heard – not even the keen of a gull. It was nearly noon but it was pitch dark – like midnight. The men realised, too late, what they had got themselves into.

They were in the path of a mighty cyclone that came out of Europe and blew in a North Easterly direction. Nearly all the Eyemouth boats turned into the teeth of it in order to try to get back home. The great storm was upon them in the blink of an eye. Most of the boats capsized amid huge seas and towering waves. Others foundered on the jagged Hurkar rocks trying to win home into the safe haven of Eyemouth harbour. In those conditions it would have been easier for a camel to get through the eye of a needle. Survivors spoke of seeing masts snapped like matchsticks by the howling gale. Only one, the *Ariel Gazelle,* tried to outrun the storm. It was blown across the North Sea almost as far as Norway. But it turned up safely at Eyemouth two days later. That day 129 fishermen from Eyemouth were lost and the total reached 189 when those lost from the neighbouring fishing communities of Burnmouth, Newhaven, Cove, Fisherrow and Coldingham Shore were taken into account. Thomas Fairbairn was one of them, hit by a half ton of water side on that took him over the gunwhales and into the cold churning sea. He came up once and was heard to shout out one word – Belle! – before his seaboots filled and a huge wave covered him. There were many acts of bravery and heroism that took place that day but none that could bring back Thomas.

The following days were grim indeed as bodies and bits of bodies, mostly unrecognisable, were washed up along the coast and taken away for burial. A relief fund was set up to help the stricken families and £50,000 pounds was raised, a huge sum in those days. Three days after the disaster a tall, thin young man with receding hair showed up at *Jonah's Neuk* and asked to speak to Belle. He introduced himself as the cousin of Thomas Fairbairn. She would already have heard the terrible news about the disaster to the North in Scotland? She had. He was afraid he had even worse news to bring of a personal nature. He was very sorry, but her fiance Thomas had been lost in the dreadful storm of the 14th. A number of survivors had testified to what they had seen. His body had not been recovered from the sea. He had almost certainly been drowned, one of the many victims of Black Friday. But Belle already knew that she had lost him. There was no need for her to sit down and take a brandy for the shock as poor Willie suggested. She had known from the second that the sky had darkened above Seahouses that day as the killing storm lowered overheard and rolled Northward to complete its evil work. A feeling of despair and the utmost dread had engulfed her there and then and she had known deep within herself that she would never see Thomas again in this life. The tall cousin of Thomas Fairbairn would return again to Seahouses – this time with a proposal of marriage for Belle. He would become known in the town subsequently as poor Willie the Scotsman . . .

Ugh! Aargh! They're back. My quiet day of reminiscing is over and the Blackberries are back sooner than expected. It's a wonder that the four wheel drive doesn't hit the close wall at the speed they drive at. The narrow lanes of Seahouses were never intended for cars of that speed and size. Now the gravel is all churned up and there are tyre tracks where the car has had to brake suddenly. Mrs. Blackberry and the two youngsters are turfed out before the car birls round and roars off out of the Close. Mr. Blackberry has had to break off his holiday to return to Head Office to complete a survey. He'll be back tomorrow he promises – this is just one of those things that happens in The Private Sector – he'll make up for it with presents later, he says. Mrs Blackberry is furious with her husband. He's ruined the holiday. As I gaze down on all this from the upstairs window it occurs to me that Mrs. Blackberry is more annoyed at having to look after the children on her own as much as anything else. Mr. Blackberry, as he whirled the car round, definitely had a look of relief on his face as if he was escaping something unpleasant. In fact it was a broad grin. I can understand why.

CHAPTER FOUR

Marshall Riley's Army

The Blackberries have paid Farquhair Tinkerson for the use of *Jonah's Neuk* for a week. Although I still think of it as my house, the reality is that it belongs to the Blackberries for this week – and they are entitled to behave in it just as they like, I suppose. So why is it that I find myself getting so angry with them and can't wait until they disappear back to their mono blocked estate of detached four bedroom houses? You see, it seems to me that they do not treat my old house with respect. That might seem a ridiculous thing to say. How can you treat a thing like a house – a dead old thing of bricks and pipes, crumbling mortar, arthritic wood, eyeless glass and loose slates – as if it were a living thing? I suppose what I'm saying is that they don't treat me – the invisible occupant, with respect. But how could they? – They don't know I'm here. Anyhow – they cannot seem to afford each other any respect, or other people come to that , so how might they treat things in the proper way? Young Reginald – who's main, sole purpose in life appears to be to avoid washing and all aspects of personal hygiene – refuses to take his muddy trainers off and plonks his smelly feet on the table. He circumnavigates the room by walking over the settee then jumping from chair to chair like a circus act on trampolines. Casually, he drops empty crisp packets on the floor, having spilled his crumbs down the sofa cushions. He knocks over coke cans on the carpet, smears chocolate on the cushions and he wipes his sticky hands on the curtains. None of this is so important – there are worse crimes, I suppose. I watch him behaving like this from high up on the living room wall from behind the ventilation airbrick. From time to time, if they can be bothered or are paying attention, one of his parents gives him a desultory telling off. *Pick that crisp packet up Reggie! Go and get a cloth!* He ignores them or answers back that Ronnie did it and eventually Mrs Blackberry will get up and clean up his mess. The thing is, I believe that Ronnie and Reggie take their lead from their Mum and Dad. Mr. and Mrs. Blackberry don't go around trashing the house but they continually speak in a disrespectful and disdainful way about everything and everybody, complaining and moaning and arguing. They are perpetually filling their sons' heads with the idea that they are *entitled*. Entitled to what? Well, everything, it seems. Now you might say that in the bleak, bad old days when children were expected to be seen and not heard and were expected to do whatever they were told by crazy bullying grown ups – that was much worse. It was. But I have seen a number of families in *Jonah's Neuk* since it was turned by Farqhuair Tinkerson into a holiday fun house. When it was a proper, family home there was always plenty love around here. It happed the house like cotton wool from the cold blasts of life. Sadly, that precious quality is often absent in these families. There has been a big change. What caused that to happen, I wonder?

Part of the problem seems to be an obsession with things and

I sometimes think – and this is a terrible thing to think – that little Reginald and Ronald are things or possessions as far as their parents are concerned. My evidence for this is that there is little else that they seem interested in or motivated by other than gathering up – stuff, I suppose.

When Mr. Blackberry gets back from Head Office the next day he is obliged to pull something big out of the hat so the family head off West for a day exploring Hadrian's Wall and Vindolanda. Ronnie and Reggie return home with a pile of plastic Roman stuff: helmets, swords, breast plates, toy soldiers, colouring – in books, you name it, much of it like the wall itself, already ruined and broken. Mrs. Blackberry is indignant about how a cross elderly man has told her boys off as they queued for lunch. The boys have impeccable manners I'll admit – you'll never catch Mrs. Blackberry out on that one. The only problem is that they believe that as long as they shout out *excuse me! very* loudly, they are allowed to push and shove in front of everyone else. Mrs Blackberry thinks like this as well. After all, her boys are *entitled*. We don't live in the dark ages anymore and children are entitled to express themselves, to express their opinions and to voice their likes and dislikes. She pulls a cross face and asks who the horrible old man thought he was, talking to her children like that. He had no right to even address them – they're children after all – and she would have been well within her rights to complain to a policeman.

I miss the old days greatly and particularly the parliament of hoose daemons that used to meet up on the slippery roofs and windy neuks of Seahouses. They were always lively occasions and you always went away with something to think and ruminate over. One of the liveliest of talkers, debaters, arguers and interrupters was Wee Lingy. Lingy was fascinated by all human activities – in particular politics, history and philosophy. He would describe himself as a *communist* or *socialist* and he was always keen to explain what these words meant as far as he was concerned. He said that he had taken part in the Jarrow Hunger March in nineteen thirty six when unemployed men from the North East had marched all the way to London to protest about their conditions – however he had not been able to complete the march to its final destination in London. As he travelled further and further South, particularly after he left the boundaries of Northumberland, he found himself feeling increasingly weak and dizzy. True enough, he was fading away to nothing. The further South he travelled, his powers were decreasing at a commensurate rate. He said that from the minute he had turned round and began to head for home he felt immediately better and his strength and vigour had started to come back. Wee Lingy had another interesting observation from this adventure. "Noo – listen up, bonnie lads, it's naw ivry hoose that haes its ain hoose daemon, ye knaw like? The further Sooth ye gan, the fewer hoose daemons there are for tae see, in fact, I hae ma doubts that there'll be any o the gadgies ataa by the time ye reach as faur as Lunnon. They divn't hae them there. Tell me this – hiv ye ivir met a hoose daemon fae Essex or Surrey? Mibbe there's yae or twae o them stoattin aboot doon there but there's no hunners o them like ye hae up here in God's Ain Country."

By Saint Cuthbert's Beads! exclaimed Wullie Whitebait, when Lingy had finished.

Hawhey, Man! Bollocks! shouted the other hoose daemons in derision but Lingy stuck to his guns. He had a theory.

"Certain conditions are required tae encourage the creation and habitation o hoose daemons. They divn't hiv them in the Sooth, Man. Tae hiv a hoose daemon ye maun hiv a hoose first. I mean a proper hoose like. And whit is a hoose? Weel, I'll tell yous aa noo, ma bonny lads. A hoose is a canny wee boatie that divn't seems to move ataa. Tak a swadge at it – it seems anchored fast. Beached. But naw – a hoose – a good gaun hoose at any rate like – is mair than bricks and mortar. It's an ark. An ark o souls. And although it divn't seems tae budge an inch, it sails in time.

If you might watch it – tak a right guid keek at it ower a hunner years or so – you'd aye see it moving. I believe that at yae time ivry hoose, though nae maitter hoo humble or smaa, had it's ain hoose daemon tae guide it and look oot for it's crew and cargo, its hearth and roof tree. The sad thing is – human folk divn't think o their hooses in these terms nae longer like. Their hoose is just mair money in the bank tae them, another possession, a thing. For a lang time they thought they had forgotten us. But there was aye somebody wi a mindin o Hoose daemons at the back o their memory. Noo there is naebody, Bonnie lads. We're the last, I trow. We dae weel tae keep the boatie afloat amang oorsels but the time is coming and it'll no be lang afore aal the attic spaces are lown and the chimney stacks are empty o snoring hoose daemons hivin a bit kip in the efternoon.

Later I asked Roller skate to find out about the Jarrow March for me, and this is what he told me in his dry way: "Ahem – well now, young Tammy Norrie – *The Jarrow March* or *Jarrow Crusade,* from the phrase on banners carried by the marchers, was an October 1936 protest march against unemployment and extreme poverty suffered in North East England during the Great Depression – ahem, which you will remember well enough yourself. The 207 marchers travelled from the town of Jarrow to the Palace of Westminster in London, a distance of almost 300 miles, to lobby Parliament. Their MP, Ellen Wilkinson, known as 'Red Ellen', walked with them. Ahem, when the marchers completed their feat, very little was done for them. The town's shipbuilding industry remained closed, with the marchers given £1 each for the train fare back from London.The march was to find jobs to support Jarrow men and their families. It was also a bid for respect and recognition, not only for the people of Jarrow, ahem, but for others in a similar situation all over the country. The marchers had no resources other than their own determination, and some good boots supplied by the public. During the march, wherever the marchers stopped for the night, the local people gave them shelter and food.

The marchers were selected carefully, with only fit men being allowed to participate. A separate march of 200 blind people also left for London in October 1936. The marchers were supported by a bus which carried cooking equipment and ground sheets for when the march had to stop outside. Many of the men marched in army style, walking for fifty minutes before a ten-minute break, and they held blue and white banners. A harmonica band and frequent singing helped to keep the morale of the marchers high.

The original petition, which demanded government aid for the town of Jarrow, signed by 11,000 people from the town, was carried in an oak box, whilst supporters of the March could add to an additional petition. The marchers spent the nights in local accommodation, whilst sometimes receiving extra aid from locals. For example, ahem, in Barnsley, the marchers were allowed to use the specially-heated Municipal Baths – pay attention now, young Tammy – after all, ahem, you did ask for this information.

The marchers arrived in London on 31 October, almost a month after leaving. The petition was handed into Parliament by Wilkinson. The Prime Minister of the day, Stanley Baldwin, refused to see any of the marchers' representatives, claiming it would set a dangerous precedent. The marchers generally received sympathy, though no proposal was made to help Jarrow, despite the petition being accepted in the House of Commons — with a single simple sentence of announcement, after which the House of Commons went back to their previous business. Hansard reveals to us that the march was also discussed at Prime Minister's Questions on the 5th of November, 1936.

It was not until two years after the Jarrow March, in 1938, that a ship breaking yard and engineering works were established in Jarrow. The next year a steelworks was established. However the depression continued in Jarrow until after the beginning of World War 2 in September 1939, when industrial production increased due to the nation's need for re-armament. When wars come along employment generally improves.

The Jarrow March is fondly remembered by those on the left in British politics as a landmark in the history of the labour movement, even though, ahem, the Labour Party of the day opposed it, and the Trades Union Congress circularised Trades Councils advising them not to help the marchers.

The last surviving member of the march, Cornelius Whalen, died on 14 September 2003, at the age of 93. Ahem."

Thank you, Roller Skate.

CHAPTER FIVE

We Can Swing Together

A century before the Jarrow Crusade, young Grace Darling was not much older than Reginald when her family moved to Longstone in the Farnes. Bob Cod said she was always a quiet, determined wee thing. Nevertheless it must have been a daunting prospect for a child to go to live on a lonely lighthouse on a bleak and wild rock that only rose a few feet above the sea and which was often completely submerged in times of storms and gales. In the wintertime, when it grew dark early it must have felt particularly cut off and lonely. It was February 1826 when Grace's dad took over the job of keeper in the newly constructed lighthouse that rose from the bare rock to rise eighty feet high in the air where the gulls cry. But under the conditions of the day imposed by the Corporation of Trinity House, who were in charge of all lighthouses around the British coast, the whole

Darling family had to be responsible for keeping this beacon of hope in the North alight. It was a big responsibility, for all kinds of ships had been foundering and sailors' lives and merchants' fortunes had been lost on the treacherous rocks of the Farnes for as long as there had been ships and sailors and merchants.

Bob Cod said he could remember the earliest attempts at providing warnings to sailors who had got themselves into trouble in these dangerous waters. At first, these had been little more than big bonfires of coal and driftwood set afire on the tops of stone towers on the inner, more accessible islands. Before Longstone was built there had been such a tower on Brownsman. They were not always visible and the light they created did not travel a long way. But Longstone was further out and for its time it was a state of the art wonder. It had a revolving light with reflectors of silvered copper. The base contained the kitchen living room, and as it tapered upwards and narrowed there were three successively smaller bedrooms, the second of which, twelve feet in diameter, was Grace's. Outbuildings huddled round the lighthouse itself including the boathouse and the oil store and a tank that collected rainwater for drinking, washing and cooking. Grace's dad even kept a small garden and livestock on a neighbouring island that he would row out to to attend – from time to time a storm would come along and lift it and its occupants away in their entirety. State of the art or not it must have been a lonely, cold, damp, and dangerous place for Grace and her brothers to be brought up. One careless slip on the wet rocks and you could be in the deep cold sea drowning. But for Grace's father it was a reasonably well paid job that enabled him to look after his family at a time of great economic hardship in the North East. It was from the deep recessed window in her bedroom that Grace looked out into the darkness at around a quarter to five am on the stormy morning of 7th September, 1836 and saw the wreck of the steamship *Forfarshire*, its back broken on the West point of the Harker rock about 400 yards away from Longstone. Or at least, that's one version of the story . . .

A great wail of anguish like a soul in torment has just emitted from the bathroom followed by piteous cries of 'Mummy! Mummy!" Although loud enough to wake the dead themselves it is not sufficient to disturb Mr. Blackberry who rolls over on his side and continues with his snoring. Ronald is not one to give up easily once embarked upon a strenuous voyage of attention seeking and the tremulous calls keep up in intensity until Mrs. Blackberry rises from her fitful slumbers. Normally, at this hour of the morning I'm up and about, getting ready for my early dook in the freezing and refreshing incoming tide down on the deserted grey beach. However this particular morning I'm looking forward to a long lie, having been up most of the night haunting the house and trying to spook the Blackberries. I'm particularly cross, having just curled up in my cosy neuk, cuddling Nicey, and having just crossed over into that warm land of grey and pink dreams, when I'm rudely pulled back into the cold reality of dawn. Having said that, I'm to blame to some extent. During the night I have been working overtime, pushing water up and down the plumbing system, partly to make noises that will keep the guests awake and make them believe that there are malevolent spirits at work within the walls of *Jonah's Neuk,* and partly to create nasty surprises when the guests decide to take a shower or use the toilet and are overcome with gushes of freezing cold water where none should occur. It's tiring work pushing gallons of water through narrow pipes in the middle of the night when you should be sleeping. Ronnie, wide awake and bored, has been up and about early. Wandering into the bathroom, he has climbed up onto the edge of the bath and invented a great new game – a kind of arial runway, involving leaping from the edge of the bath, grabbing a handful of shower curtain and swinging along merrily for a few feet or so until crashing into the wall and sliding down the bath's side. I sometimes wonder about Ronald's level of intelligence – Mrs. Blackberry is convinced that he has a far above average IQ level and that he is destined for great things as a doctor (due to his caring side) or as an inventor (because of his scheming mind) who will improve the lot of mankind in unimaginable ways in future days. Mr. Blackberry is convinced he will play for Man. United. I believe that Mrs. Blackberry may have received erroneous information as Ronnie seems incapable of establishing a connection between cause and consequence. For the first couple of shots the runway works fine and dandy before the inevitable happens and the shower rail buckles and collapses under Ronnie's weight. He fairly stots off the hard edge of the bath before toppling inside, slithering up and down the smooth edges like he is bob – sleighing down the Cresta Run. He ends up wedged in tightly between the two taps, bruised and somewhat dazed. Normally in such a situation, Ronnie, understanding very quickly that he has broken the shower curtain and is therefore in trouble with his Dad, will pick himself up without a murmur and slope off back to bed, denying all knowledge of the shower curtain at a later time with raised eyebrows, hurt eyes, open mouthed astonishment and indignant pose, as he blames his brother. But it's the indignity that does it more than the pain. A quart of freezing cold water that I have carefully left emits from the shower head on to Ronnie below. Then the two taps cough out another few complimentary pints in sympathy. It's all too much and isn't fair for Ronnie, sitting in a squelchy puddle on the bottom of the bath, sore, bruised and soaked with his Wayne Rooney tracksuit ruined. "Mummy! Mummy!" He wails.

Understandably, Mrs Blackberry is not happy with the situation. I hear her scolding Ronnie but it is clear that her words are being spoken loudly enough for her husband to hear. But he doesn't – he snores on. Instead it is I who cannot get to sleep. Mrs. Blackberry's voice has a high pitched nasal atonal quality that is nevertheless very piercing – and it goes on and on even though I end up plugging my ears up in the attic with bits of woolly old pipe lagging. Individual words and phrases intrude. "Really not good enough . . . this is turning into a holiday from hell . . . time you began to behave in a responsible way . . . I blame that awful school . . . why did you knock over that wine glass as well? . . . (Yipee!, that one didn't quite work out but still a result, of sorts) . . . could have killed yourself . . . I'll be speaking to the owner . . . bloody awful place . . . who leaves a shower curtain like that to tempt children ? . . . not a safe environment at all . . . bloody awful plumbing as well . . . Mark, I insist you get on the phone and demand a refund . . . Mark! Did you hear what I said? . . ."

Zzzzzzzzzzzzzzzsnort! Eventually I nod off into sleepy slumbers and leave them to enjoy their morning bickering. I fall into a deep sleep, dreaming about the house the way it was in the old days.

When Old Hilda – who was still quite young in those days – and young Bert – who was not so young as all that, moved into *Jonah's Neuk,* life continued pretty much as it had always had. The same routine, the same things. I like that. In those days people kept houses the same. There was certainly no money to build an extension or knock down a wall to put up a conservatory or an extra bedroom. But I don't think anybody saw the need to change something back then that was perfectly adequate and served its purpose. Folk should be careful when they set about ripping out the insides of houses and replacing and rebuilding. The soul of a house is very fragile and if alterations are carried out in an unthoughtful way and without due respect all kinds of disturbing ramifications can occur in an injured house. The daunting presence of Belle was missed but her things were still there to remind us of her and time passed and we treasured her life in memory and thought. I was still a young hoose daemon in those days, scampering and whizzing about the place, very nosey and into everything. But already enormous changes were happening. The railway line had reached Seahouses long before but I remember the terrifying moment of seeing the first smoking growling automobile bumping and trundling along the rutted lane. In fact, the shuddering beast nearly ran right into me as I flew around the corner. I could not believe it – Roller Skate had spoken solemnly to us of horseless carriages whose wheels were powered by gears and pistons set in motion by igniting petroleum under pressure but we had not taken him seriously. And this thing was going so fast – at least 4 miles per hour. But other changes were on the way – and not all of them good either. Great upheavals lay in store.

One of the good changes that happened at this time was that once again *Jonah's Neuk* had a bairn living in it again. For Hilda and Bert brought with them a daughter – a lovely wee thing, with big wide wise grey eyes that glinted and sparkled like the sunlight on rock pools. She was, of course, Young Hilda and I was captivated by her from the moment I first saw her. She was a good babby too – she never cried or grew fractious for no reason. From the very beginning Young Hilda was special, having about her a timeless quality. She lay quietly in her cradle in *Jonah's Neuk* looking out at the world with those big wise eyes while outside in the world beyond our little fishing hamlet rumours grew of a war on an unprecedented scale.

The remarkable thing about the babby Hilda was that for such a vivacious, inquisitive and wise beyond her years child her parents were very average and non – descript. Old Hilda was a quiet, tight – lipped woman who went about her work showing no emotion at all of either joy or vexation. You could call her dour. She said little and seldom passed an opinion about anything. You would never have known that her mother had been the fierce and ferocious Belle, scourge of landlords and skippers. Old Hilda did inherit her mother's physical strength and capacity for continuous work. Bert I never much cared for. Not because he was an evil or nasty man – quite the opposite. It was hard to have any feelings about Bert – it was like there was nothing there. He was of medium height and build, had no outstanding features to speak of physically apart from a sandy moustache of the type that all the men had back then. Sometimes he had a bit of a stammer which probably made him self conscious and he had a nervous silly laugh – like he was bemused by everything and thought the world was a slightly silly joke or puzzle that had been sprung on him. He sort of hung about the house and went out to work when it was time along with the other fishermen. If he had a few coppers he would go to the pub and have a few pints but he never changed, even with a drink in him. He stayed clear of fights, betting and gambling or drinking to excess. He handed over most of his pay to Old Hilda and he provided for his baby daughter so I suppose he was a dutiful husband and father. However after all these years his memory does not leave a deep impression and I have difficulty in recalling him clearly.

When the war started in August 1914 Bert was already in his forties. Never one to read a newspaper or become unduly involved in local affairs let alone international events, the whole thing might have been a football or rugby international taking place over a weekend in London as far as Bert was concerned. A man in a pub once told him the news that the *Titanic* had hit an iceberg and sunk. When he came home he told Old Hilda, "I hear a Sunderland chap wor drooned at sea." In fact, I can remember him clearly stating to Hilda that "This war thingy's got n – nowt to do with us, m – ma hinny." One of the few definite statements I can recall him making on the subject of international affairs. One day in the back yard a neighbour mentioned the Great War that was going on in France and asked if Bert had heard any news. "They're certainly getting a n – nice day for it," said Bert. Bert's lack of interest in the War was the opposite from the heated and animated discussion that took place at the time on the roof tiles of Seahouses as the various hoose daemons debated the ins and outs, wrongs and rights of it. Bob Cod said that he wished he was a human so that he might enlist and go and sort the damn Huns out. Why, he might even head over the sea to Belgium to take a bit look for himself. Wee Billy Ling claimed that it was a capitalist war as all wars necessarily are and that pacifism was the only response that was justifiable.

However, two years later, one windy, sunny day, when Old Hilda and young Hilda had gone to the drying green to hang out the washing, Bert crept into the house surreptitiously and with some difficulty began to scrawl a note on a scrap of paper. He quickly grabbed a bag of things that he had already prepared – it was the kit bag he usually took to sea with him – and slipped out the door. I had been trying to squint over Bert's shoulder – it was highly unusual to see him write anything. So unusual I didn't even know he could. The note said: Dear Hilda am gone to do my bit. See you latter on. Yours Bert.

This was an enormous surprise and came out of the blue. Bert had gone to Tynemouth and volunteered for the Durham Light Infantry Regiment. Old Hilda came in, picked up the note, read it and sighed. "Stupid man!". Then she crumpled it up and flung it in the fireplace. Then she started emptying the washing basket as if nothing had happened. What motivated Bert to join up? Certainly there was a lot of pressure in society at the time put upon able men to enlist. But Bert was of an age and in a job where he didn't need to. Certainly the old sailors raised a glass of rum to good old patriotic Bert in the *Forfarshire Lounge* but I think the answer is that he simply became bored with life as a fisherman and fancied going abroad for a change of scenery and lifestyle. He never struck anybody as a King and Country man. Bert went through his basic training and was quickly sent to the Front in France. This was just after the terrible battle of the Somme where the British Army had lost so many men and they needed soldiers badly. From time to time a letter would come back – usually brief and not very often.

Meanwhile Young Hilda was growing up in her father's absence. From the start she was different from all the other bairns in Seahouses. For one thing, she refused to eat fish from a young age despite the protestations and exhortations of her mum. The other thing that singled her out was her love of books. There weren't many to be had in *Jonah's Neuk* but what Young Hilda liked better than anything was reading. She would sit on a little wooden stool by the fireplace and be transported away to the worlds of the imagination. She even read Belle's battered old bible from cover to cover at one point. She loved going to school. At that time, it was common for working class children to be kept off school by their parents to help in the house or even with work. The education of most children ended when somewhere between the ages of twelve and fourteen by which time, if they had been lucky, they would have a rudimentary knowledge of how to read, write and count – like Bert. Young Hilda loved school because there were books there – some of which she was allowed to borrow and bring home. She also befriended the Doctor's daughter and was given the loan of books from his small library – the same library that Roller Skate dipped into often. While she took part in the same skipping games and street rituals as the other bairns she also kept herself apart – there was a side to young Hilda that few saw but me. She helped her mother with the household chores but there was a glowing golden light in Young Hilda's grey eyes – like sunlight in rock pools.

One afternoon in summer Old Hilda was in a bad mood. Unusually, she was very grumpy and her normal dour taciturnity spilled over into bad temper. You could tell she wasn't happy. She muttered under her breath, complaining about the war, the lack of things in the local shops, not having a man about the house to help her. I was curled up on the window sill dozing and keeping one eye on Young Hilda, who as usual, was sitting on a stool by the fire with her nose in a book. Old Hilda was in the kitchen and you could hear her clattering pots and banging cupboard doors too hard. Then she dropped a cup and it smashed and there was a lot of fuss and complaining. The cup smashing woke me up a bit but Young Hilda kept on reading, oblivious. The Doctor's daughter had given her a loan of a book called *Jayne Eyre* and she was utterly captivated and transported by it. Her grey eyes widened in enthrallment and she was obviously transported to another place and time as she read. In came Old Hilda:

"Huh! Nose in a book again!" But Young Hilda wasn't listening. "No use them."

"Eh?" said Young Hilda, looking up.

"Why don't you get out in the fresh air with the other lassies? You're always sitting about in the house reading. It's not good for a young lassie." Old Hilda went on. Usually, she said little even when she was annoyed – her lips would get a little tighter and form a prim straight line – but that was the only sign. Today she had had enough.

"But Ma – I like reading." said Young Hilda.

"Books'll not get you a husband. Who do you think you are? When I was your age I was helping Belle bait hooks. Do you think you're better than us? The Doctor's lass will be going to school in Edinburgh soon. That's not for you – so best put it out of your head. We're poor. We have to work. Make yourself useful girl – if you're not going out then you can help me make fishcakes from these old cod heads." Then Old Hilda stumped out.

Young Hilda was furious. A solitary tear streaked down her face which had turned a beetroot colour. I felt so sorry for her – it was clear to me, that at a tender young age, it was as if she had just seen her hopes of a better future and her dreams of a different world cruelly torn up in front of her. She could not see me so I could not help her. All I could do was lie there on the sill and smile sympathetically at her, hoping that my good wishes would reach her at some level and provide some subconscious consolation for her. Suddenly Young Hilda picked up *Wuthering Heights* and hurled it in my direction in a blind fury. I moved like lightening as it whizzed past my head, missing me by inches, and cracked the window pane behind me.

"And what are you grinning at Beastie, you horrible, sneaky, snaky eely thing?" Young Hilda hissed at me. "Do you think it's funny or something? That's right, clear off you pest and stay away from me!"

I was dumbfounded. Young Hilda could see me! She had aways seen me from the time she was a babby, cooing and gurgling in her cradle. I fairly whizzed up the chimney and made myself as small as I could, trembling like a baby bird and trying to figure out this astonishing news that had instantly transformed my world. She had been able to see me all the time! But she had never ever given any indication – or had she perhaps and I just hadn't noticed? If Young Hilda could see me, were there perhaps others humans? My head was spinning with unanswered questions. I had to speak with the other Hoose Daemons about this extraordinary turn of events . . .

Chasing away a group of annoying pigeons away first, we met up on the roof of the Old Fish Smokery on a still balmy evening when the town had quietened down and I recounted the extraordinary events of the day to my fellow hoose daemons. "By Saint Cuthbert's Beads!" exclaimed Wullie Whitebait, when I had finished. Then for once, there was silence among that quarrelsome group before Roller Skate spoke.

"Ahem. This is indeed momentous news. It is exceedingly rare for a human being to be able to see a hoose daemon and particularly to be able to communicate with one. In the modern era there have only been a handful of cases recorded in Daemon lore. In the past -ahem – I'm going back over a thousand years ago – it was much more common. Many of the early Celtic saints and monks apparently had this ability although they were not always well disposed toward our kind. Ahem, for example, History records the Irish monk Columba exorcising one of our kind from a broch on the shores of Loch Ness. While dependent upon a symbiotic relationship with humans ever since they first developed the habit of home dwelling, our relationship with Christianity has not always been ahem, a positive one. The increasing inability of humans to recognise our presence has in fact allowed us to get on with our work in peace. In nearly all cases, we can see them but they cannot see us. More recently a number of groups of animals have also lost the ability to see us also although mostly they are still aware of our existence. However – ahem – even in this late period in our history, there are precedented cases – admittedly rare – of ahem, exceptionally gifted human individuals who have retained the perceptional abilities to see us. It seems from what Young Tammy has told us that Young Hilda is such a one."

Roller Skate continued: "You are not to worry about this, Young Tammy. In fact, You must regard this as a benison. In all recorded cases of this happening, the human perceivers have tended to be not only exceptionally gifted individuals but also extremely sensitive, intelligent and empathetic ones. In other words, Young Hilda is not likely to betray you to other humans. She realises that only she can see you and to reveal your presence would only cause her distress as other humans would consider her mad or seeking attention. If she was going to , ahem, reveal you, she would have done so before now."

At this point, Old Crabby Pincer, who rarely ever spoke, winced and grimaced and finally began to splutter, his pop eyes bulging out from under his shelly head. And because he very rarely said anything, everyone knew to be quiet because it would be worth listening.

"Hrrrp – Hrrp Baa," girned Old Pincer.

"What's that? What's that he's saying?" demanded Harry Haddock, "I can't make it out."

"Say it again, Pincer," asked Bob Cod.

"Hrrrp – Hrrp Baa," emitted Old Pincer again.

"I've got it!" said Seabasstian,"It's something about a herring bone – have you choked on one, Pincer?" But Pincer shook his head. Then he nodded.

"I remember now," shouted Harry, " Herring Bone – do you remember Roller Skate? He used to come around every now and again. A morose chap – always fed up, with a runny nose and a cough. A real loner. Haven't seen him in decades."

"Aye – right enough," exclaimed Bob Cod, "He was the Darlings' Hoose Daemon out on Longstone. Always moaning. Either that or chuntering on about little Grace."

And so it turned out that there had been a hoose daemon biding out there on that little rocky isle in that cold drafty lighthouse – for not only was it a lighthouse but a home as well for the Darling family. And what was extraordinary was the fact that in later years when, driven by loneliness and isolation, the old daemon had made the sea crossing over to Seahouses to seek some companionship, Herring Bone, the Longstone Lighthouse daemon, had claimed that young Grace Darling had not only been able to see him but to communicate with him. The Parliament of Cronies had been skeptical but Herring Bone had repeated this claim on many occasions. Barely remembered, he had not been seen around since families stopped living on Longstone. Like many since, it was conjectured that he had gone to *Fiddler's Green*.

And so I heard from the Hoose Daemons the Herring Bone version of events on 7th September, 1838. *The Forfarshire* was a state of the art steamship – at this time the majority of ships still had sails. Launched in Dundee in 1834 and owned by The Dundee, Perth and London Shipping company, she was powered by two ninety horse power engines that could help her reach a top speed of eight knots. She was a luxury passenger vessel, built with wooden planks over an iron framework but she could also transport up to four hundred tons of cargo. She had sailed from Hull on the 5th of September with sixty three souls – crew and passengers on board, including Captain Humble and his wife, bound for her home port of Dundee. She nearly got there, steaming head first into a gale and huge swelling seas. But the steam engines had been playing up and labouring in the rolling seas all the way up the East coast. A leak was discovered but the pumps could not clear the boiling scalding water in order for it to be fixed. Eventually, off Saint Abb's Head both engines had to be shut down. The emergency sails were hauled up but in the tremendous gale the ship began to drift South. The skipper was trying to guide The *Forfarshire* into the sanctuary of the inner Farnes but he got it wrong. The ship struck the Big Harcar rock just four hundred yards away from the comparative safety of Longstone Lighthouse. But on that night, in those seas, it may as well have been a hundred miles away.

The traditional story goes that Grace saw the wreck on the rocks from her bedroom window before five in the morning. It was not until nearer seven that she saw figures moving on that slippery promontory and realised that there had been survivors. The Victorian sentimental version then paints us a picture of Grace exhorting her elderly father to row out to the rock with her in a tiny cobble to rescue the nine survivors. This story became enshrined in the Victorian consciousness and Grace went on to become a lauded and famous heroine like Florence Nightingale.

As always there is a grain of truth in the story but much has been added on. For one thing, Grace was undoubtedly a brave lassie but there was no way she was capable of rowing out to the wreck on her own – the fact was, her elder brothers were all away from home on the mainland. One of them had been out drinking in the Seahouses' pubs. Grace's Dad, William was a canny lad and a very brave man. It was his decision to set out, with young Grace to help him, to rescue the survivors, as he had done many times before in his distinguished career.

How could Grace have seen the wreck in the dark at that time, amid the spray and the thundering massive waves? The lighthouse logbook tells us that her mother had been on watch during the latter part of the night but had seen nothing amiss. It was, according to Herring Bone, who had been curled up asleep on the window ledge recess, no more than a trembling in the air detected by his sensitive gills. A dull dream that woke him of a splintering whine and grinding crash that somehow reached his senses above the scream of the wind. Knowing that something was far wrong Herring Bone had scampered up the winding staircase and fairly whizzed up the near vertical ladder that led to the reflector room. Peering into the murky night sky, he had seen *the Forfarshire,* broken-backed on the pitiless rock. Herring Bone leapt out of the lighthouse into the swirling darkness and hurled himself off the nearly submerged rock into the heaving waters and battled through the waves across the four hundred yards to find out if there were survivors. He counted nine, frozen, shocked and huddled together on the rain and wind lashed rock. There were bodies too and one woman cradled two dead children in her arms. They were silent, too exhausted and disorientated to cry out for help. Herring Bone knew that there was little time left to save them. He turned back and swam back to the lighthouse, keeping his head beneath the hurtling waves and knowing that the swelling sea might crash him to pieces against the jagged rocks at any time. It was Herring Bone who, soaked and bedraggled, woke up Grace and desperately attempted to communicate what had happened to her. This used up further energy. Eventually, by flying up to the window and pointing and flicking his tail, he managed to get his message across. Rubbing her eyes and grumbling, Grace got up to see what the fuss was about. At first she could see nothing through the rain spattered thick glass. "Is there something there?" she asked. Herring Bone nodded. "Is it a boat?" He nodded. "Are there people out there?" And that is how Grace was able to tell her father about the wrecked ship.

But it was Grace's father who took the decision to set out in the little cobble to rescue the survivors. Grace's mother helped them launch the tiny fragile thing from the semi-submerged slipway. This time Herring Bone sat in the boat. He said it took them ages to row across in the rough seas and when they got to Harker rock, by his account, he played a major part. Grace's Dad William had to leap from the boat on to the slimy rock. While Grace kept the boat steady, Herring Bone had already gone back into the water and caught William's foot as it slipped on the rock. According to Herring Bone the old lighthouse keeper never knew that his life had been saved by him. It took two journeys to get all the survivors back to Longstone and on both trips Herring Bone had to swim back all the way.

Later on the North Sunderland lifeboat arrived. Nine further survivors had been picked up further South in a lifeboat. Herring Bone always complained that the terrible cold he caught that day from being drenched in the North Sea for so long had never ever left him. He had a runny nose and a cough ever after . . .

When the story was finished Wullie Whitebait made his usual timeworn exclamation. "By Saint Cuthbert's Beads!" he gasped.

"Tell me Roller Skate," I asked, "I've always wanted to know – What exactly are Saint Cuthbert's Beads?"

"Well now young Thomas – Ahem – St. Cuthbert's beads (or Cuddy's beads as we say in the informal colloquial habit) are fossilised portions of the stems of Carboniferous crinoids. Crinoids are a kind of marine echinodem which are still extant, and which are sometimes known as *sea lilies*. These bead-like fossils are washed out onto the beach and in medieval Northumberland were strung together as necklaces and rosaries and became associated with St Cuthbert.

In other parts of England circular crinoid columnals were known as *fairy money*, while pentagonal crinoid columnals were known as *star stones*, and moulds of the stems left impressions which were known as *screwstones*.

Ahem – speaking in terms of Paleontology – which as you know is something of a hobby of mine – the so called *beads* are in fact – ahem – thick discs or short cylinders which, when the crinoid was still alive, were articulated to form a branched structure, linked by soft tissue, nerves and ligaments which occupied the central hole, known as the *lumen*. The columnals usually became disarticulated after the animal died. Articulated crinoid fossils are relatively rare, but disarticulated columnals are quite common in the fossil record. They may be extracted from their matrix, often limestone or, in the case of exposures in coastal cliffs, they can sometimes be found washed out of the matrix and deposited on the foreshore as if from the sea.

Ahem – but getting back to history and lore – in medieval Northumberland, the fossilised columnals, as I said, were collected at Lindisfarne and strung together as a necklace or rosary. Over time, they became associated with St. Cuthbert, who was a monk on Lindisfarne and the nearby island of Hobthrush also known as St Cuthbert's Isle. St Cuthbert, in the 7th century became Bishop of Lindisfarne. According to legend, it was said that St. Cuthbert used the beads as a rosary, or that his spirit created them on stormy nights so they could be found on the beach the next morning. The first known reference to Cuthbert's beads in a documentary source is found in an account of a visit to Lindisfarne by a certain John Ray in 1671. Ahem – in literature, in Sir Walter Scott's famous poem *Marmion,* written in 1808, St. Cuthbert is described by fishermen as creating these bead-like fossils. Incidentally, the poem also makes reference to St Hilda of Whitby, Yorkshire who, according to religious legend, turned snakes into stone, the *snake stones* being the numerous fossil ammonites of that area.

> But fain Saint Hilda's nuns would learn
> If, on a rock by Lindisfarne,
> Saint Cuthbert sits, and toils to frame
> The sea-born beads that bear his name:
> Such tales had Whitby's fishers told
> And said they might his shape behold,
> And here his anvil sound:
> A deadened clang – a huge dim form
> Seen but and heard when gathering storm
> And night were closing round.
> But this, a tale of idle fame,
> The nuns of Lindisfarne disclaim.

Ahem – thanks for that Tammy. It's not often that I get the chance to show off my learning – what's the vulgar expression? Ahem, yes – strut my stuff. So I always welcome your enquiries for that reason. You are and always have been remarkable and different as well as inquisitive – which is why, you know, you were named after a seabird when the other daemons were given fish names. "

Thanks for that too, Roller Skate. Now I have a clue what Wullie's on about. It's all he ever says so I should at least try to understand it.

So now I knew that Young Hilda could see me. That she had seen me all along and there had been other instances in the past where human beings had been able to see and communicate with Hoose Daemons. Roller Skate did warn me however that this state of affairs with Young Hilda might not always last – as time went on, sometimes humans lost the gift completely or partially. When I returned to *Jonah's Neuk* I became a lot more shy and coy when young Hilda was around. I would often hide or bolt up the chimney when she came into a room. Young Hilda thought this was funny and I would hear her chuckling away to herself. "Away you go then, Beastie," she would say.

"What's that you're saying Young Hilda?" her mother would ask.

"I'm talking to the cat, Ma," said Young Hilda.

"Don't be stupid girl – cats can't understand."

"Oh – they can, Ma. Believe me. Ghostly sea snaky cats can!"

One morning in late March there was a knock on the front door. A boy stood, nervously holding a yellow telegram. Old Hilda came to the door with the kitchen knife in her hand. She took it and closed the door without a word. In the kitchen, she opened it and read it. It said that Young Bert was missing in action and was presumed dead. He had been serving as part of 50th Northumbrian Division in the 2nd Battalion of The Durham Light Infantry at a place in France named Qveant – Pronville. There had been a terrible battle. Only two officers and twenty five soldiers had survived. Young Bert would never return home to *Jonah's Neuk*. Old Hilda scrunched the telegram up in her fist and flung it in the bucket. "Oh foolish man," she whispered and continued slicing onions for the soup. She wiped a solitary tear from her eye with the back of her hand. When she heard the news, Young Hilda was distraught and sobbed and sobbed and sobbed. For months after I would hear her cry herself to sleep at night as I lay curled up, half way up the chimney.

CHAPTER SIX

Dingly Dell

Tyr – Odin – Thor – Freya: Thank the Gods that the Blackberries' week at *Jonah's Neuk* is almost over and soon I will have the old house to myself again. I can hardly wait. Farquhair Tinkerson showed up this morning, summonsed by Mark's aggressive phone call to look at the dodgy shower and the wonky plumbing and the faulty wiring and the drafty bedroom and the kettle that switches itself on by itself and the heating that switches itself off by itself and the poor sound proofing that lets strange noises at night disturb families trying to enjoy a well earned break after working hard all year, etc. I knew Farquhair was here because I noticed, when I woke up, not one but two over – large, ugly cars squeezed into the forecourt, parked nose to nose against each other like competing angry rhinos. Those kind of cars that should look like normal sized cars only someone has inflated them with a bicycle pump to twice the volume. Or their owners have been feeding their car steroids in its petrol drink like the body builders imbibe. I have noticed that if humans have a defect of smallness of some kind – in intelligence, bigness of heart or kindness of spirit – they tend to make up for it by hiding behind masques of large things whether it be psychopathic dogs, stupid cars or gross houses. Although I am physically very small this kind of thinking plays no part in my philosophy. I have spent my years trying to enlarge my soul only.

Watching the two of them enacting a kind of macho dance from just under the rones it was hard to pick out which one of the two I disliked most. I must admit it was fun to see Farqhair in his checked shirt and green waxed jacket discomfited. He grinned at Mark revealing his numerous small and even teeth in an accommodating affable manner but his pale bulging eyes popping out of his pink face balefully told a different story. How little he had changed since Doris had first brought him to see Young Hilda during the Christmas holidays of 1968. Mark was coming out with the usual blustery stuff – he would be writing to *English Country Cottages, The Northumbrian Tourist Board* and *Which Magazine* et al. He was not the sort to be pushed around. A significant discount was the least expected for ruining his children's holiday that they had been so looking forward to. He was a man of some influence and he would see to it that none of his colleagues would be using any of Farquhair's death trap properties again – on the other hand, for a free holiday he might be able to put some of his clients in touch. Eventually, they wrangled their way to some kind of agreement that suited both of their four wheel drive egos and which altered nothing whatsoever. Farqhair did agree that he would send his man round to check out the plumbing and the wiring. I knew the man he had in mind and also knew that nothing would be fixed. As he was leaving, I looked down and saw Farquhair staring up directly at me. For a second I thought that he could see me. But he couldn't. I realised that it was the house itself that he was glaring at – *Jonah's Neuk*. It was a look of disgust mixed with contempt. If he could have pulled the house down there and then and left it a heap of rubble he would have done so without a second thought. But it was still worth something to him so he couldn't.

Old Hilda was eventually granted a widow's pension of fifteen bob a week. Young Hilda was never able to fulfill her dream of going to a university and reading every novel ever written. She left school and did a variety of jobs to help supplement her Mum's meagre allowance. She worked in the old Smokery shop for many years and when times were hard she took on any extra work she could find including cleaning in the local Bed and Breakfasts and being a barmaid in The Schooner. Watching how Young Hilda's life turned out and how her exceptional gifts were wasted made me aware of how many others like her there must be. She could have done anything she set her mind to, given the chance. But too many things were against her: her sex, her position in society, the time she was born in. Most successful or rich people feel the need to believe that they have earned their position in life because they deserve it through their talent, genius or hard work. Some of them have. I can understand why most of them need to think like this – it makes them feel special, justified and entitled. But luck, of one kind or another, plays a huge part in life. People should remember that. And they should never ever believe that they are better than someone else because their house is so big they need to pay people to keep it clean. Some folk live in gilded palaces, some in glorified biscuit tins. Some poor souls have nowhere at all.

Jonah's Neuk didn't change at all much until after the Second War ended. Old Hilda lived on until 1957 and by then things like television, electricity, and later, washing machines and fridges were beginning to appear and the old ways of fishing folk were beginning to disappear. Seahouses was becoming less of a fishing harbour and more of a tourist destination. This was the start of houses beginning to be stuffed with stuff – all the clutter we believe we can no longer live without but which we lived without for years perfectly happily. Which reminds me. I must go and hide the adaptor for Mark's *i* thingy down the back of the sofa before he leaves. Of course, I know I'm an old hypocrite. The strange Goth couple who live at the end of the street have one of those TV's that take up a whole wall of their living room. And they never shut their curtains. When there's a big match on I go and perch on the opposite roof and can see the whole game free of charge. The other night Mark was complaining that *Jonah's Neuk* didn't have a Sky dish. He went out to the Forfarshire Lounge to watch the game which put him in the bad books with Mrs Blackberry. It was a bad night for Mark because his team, Man. United, were well beaten by mine, Barcelona. Apparently, it was Mrs Blackberry's "night" to have a drink, not Mark's. Everything in their relationship appears to be divided up like that from bank accounts to who buys the Big Macs for the bairns. They jealously guard their "turn" at everything to get away from their children so that they can be allowed to lead their "lives". It's pathetic. But they'll be off soon. Then it will be the Blueberries and then the Raspberries followed by some other kind of nightmareberries no doubt.

What amazes me is their lack of self awareness of what lies around them. They never ask the big questions. They never seem to ever catch the merest glimpse of the clear white light. Maybe I'm wrong – sometimes I think I think too much which is just as bad as thinking too little. However if you are hoose daemon this is inevitable. For a hoose daemon is an enigma wrapped in a riddle. It's a lonely existence with lots of time to watch and think but there's seldom anyone to talk with to answer the questions that formulate in your mind. Even less opportunity now that I am – to the best of my knowledge – the last hoose daemon left in Seahouses. Perhaps I should be following the path of the clear white light and heading into the West to find the others at Fiddler's Green. But something keeps me biding here.

What do I look like? I can't really tell because I've never seen myself. Am I ugly, comely or indifferent? I once believed that the sight of me would disturb humans which is why I was invisible to them. But the sight of me never disturbed or upset Young Hilda although she often laughed at me and called me "Beastie". I don't show up in mirrors although I think I once got a fleeting glimpse of a movement of myself in a shop window. Am I large or small? I think of myself as small always but I may be bigger at times than I think. My sense of myself is maybe different from how I seem but it is who I really am. How do I move? I wriggle, slither, roll, stack and slide. I will myself to do it and it usually happens. In the past, when I had more energy and went further afield, I would shape myself in my head into the form of a kite. On a windy day I could go far and I could even force the wind to change in my favour to take me home. What do I live on, what food sustains me? I am not going to divulge.

Who am I? Still haven't worked out that one. Who made me? I have no memory of parents. All the hoose daemons I know are blokes with no mums or dads. We're all orphans. I was formed before my memory began to function so I just have to believe that I started at some point and that i'll end at another. In my case, I have always had a strong attachment to two human made objects: a carved wooden doll whom I have always called Nicey and who I found jammed under the joists up in the darkness of the attic; secondly, a tiny and very old leather child's shoe that is hidden behind a loose brick in the chimney breast. As a young daemon Nicey was my only toy and has remained my comfort and confidant throughout. I have always felt a strong pull toward these two objects and I have an instinctive belief that they are in someway connected with the reason I am here. Roller Skate and Lingy had different theories to explain why we are here and both were quite convincing in their own way.

As I said, All the hoose daemons I know are blokes. Does that mean there are no daemon lassies? One thing I have learned about this place we inhabit is that there seems to be rules that operate. Maybe before this there were no rules and things were chaotic. A haddock might turn into a leek pudding in an instant. You might walk out the door to find the world turned upside down. Of course rules operate and take effect most of the time which is just as well. In some cases they operate not just nine times out of ten but nine trillion and ninety nine million and ninety nine thousand and ninety nine hundred and ninety nine times out of ten trillion times. But once, every now and again, out of the blue, and for no known reason, something inexplicable will happen. As soon as you think you have fixed and understood the rules in your head this over riding rule will always kick in at some point. It is worth remembering this. There will be a daemon lassie biding in a house somewhere at some point in time.

It was on that day in 1968 when Farquhair Tinkerson and Doris visited Young Hilda, by then just into her sixties and not seeing very well, that, not fancying the cut of Farquhair's gib at all let alone his little watchful piggy eyes, I decided to take myself out for the day and rolling myself into the shape of a kite, headed up to Holy Island, which was on the very furthest edge of my range. It was here on that magical tidal island that all these long years after the revelation that Hilda could see me I met the second human with this gift. It was a freezing foggy day and the air was quite still which meant flying up there took a lot of willpower. I followed the coastline for a bit up past Bamburgh Castle and then cut inland. The slipstream of the London to Edinburgh pulled me along at a good rate of knots and it was with some reluctance that I jettisoned the train and after crossing a few fields saw the up right weathered posts of the pilgrim's route that led over the ribbed and puddled squelching pale sand, seaweed-strewn, to the holy island itself. Even as late on as that there was not so much car traffic about and the island was fairly quiet excepting some tourists and a couple of wind blown bird watchers. Perhaps it had been busier earlier for already the tide was on the turn and day visitors were scurrying away clutching their bags of mead from the winery. I had a look around the Priory and admired the statue of Aiden. I thought about those early Celtic saintmen. I thought about Bob Cod. The fog was rolling in and visibility was growing quite poor. The island seemed like it was being wrapped in a tissue of yellow gauze.

I decided to head down to the castle on its little knoll. There, beside the upturned boats the fishermen use for sheds and shelters for their craft a young man was sitting on the stoney littered beach, writing with a stub of a pencil on what looked like an old school jotter. He had the look to him of what is now thought of as a "hippy" although I'm not sure if I was aware of that expression at the time. He had long brown hair that curled up into rat's tails and fell over his face, a long black greatcoat that covered most of his skinny frame and tattered old brown boots. He had a big nose that poked out from under his hair and very piercing eyes that saw a lot. It is a habit of mine, because I am invisible to most humans, that when I notice one of them reading a book or a letter or writing something my nosiness gets the better of me and I creep up close and squint over their shoulder to satisfy my curiosity. The title of what he had written got me interested straight away. But what happened next really surprised me. He was aware of my presence right away yet he neither appeared shocked or frightened.

"Aha!" he said in a gentle, slightly mocking way,"What is this that we have here? Could it be a dragon from Dreamland?" At this I was startled and turned tail. "Don't run away, little beastie – it's ok. You're not used to being seen? Stay a bit longer. I won't hurt you. You can help me finish me poem." Then he took out a fag and lit it and continued scribbling. I didn't know what to do. But there was something about him that told me it would be ok. I sidled closer and watched him. From time to time he would chat away, telling me bits and pieces about himself. I stayed there, fascinated by this strange young fellow who was able to see me, plain as day and thought nothing of it whatsoever. His name was Alan and he wrote poems and songs but not successfully. He came from Newcastle. He had been expelled from school at the age of fifteen. Back then Headmasters wielded great power and you could be asked to leave for as little as answering back to a member of staff. Alan did not strike me as the type who would keep his mouth shut if he had something to say, a question to ask or a protest to make. When he was still quite young he had been in a pop group who had won a competition, achieved some success and even released a record. But again, he had found trouble with authority, this time the record producer, and said the wrong thing at the wrong time. For a time he had worked as a window cleaner. This interested me. He had learned much looking through the soul windows of houses into folk's lives. While he continued writing his poems and playing his guitar in pubs at night he had sometimes been unemployed like the Jarrow men but he had a new job now as a nurse. This interested me too. He said it was a type of hospital where they put people who saw too much. Most of the patients are not sick at all, he told me. They're just different or unlucky or rotten things have happened to them in their lives. Some are there because they ask awkward questions in one way or another. Most are there because they see things that most people don't. They're not mad at all. There's no such thing. Many of them would see you clearly, no problems. The doctors give them drugs – sometimes so they can see less, sometimes to control what they see, sometimes just to make them sleep all day and stop shouting. But the drugs are not very good – I should know, he told me, because I've tried most of them. In the interest of science, you know? He said this with a twinkle in his eye. That's maybe why I can see you, he told me. "Tell me, beastie, are you real? Where do you live – Dingly Dell? And tell me – am I real?"

He finished writing his poem, which was titled "The Clear White Light". Suddenly he got up. "I've got to go now, Beastie –

for a pint of Guiness and to see some canny lads who want me to play in their band. Wish me luck." And he was off just like that, fading into the cold fog as if he did this kind of thing everyday. I often wonder what happened to Alan – did his life turn out like Young Hilda's, with all his youthful genius and hope thwarted by circumstance? Or was he able to fulfill his dreams? Maybe he did. I hope so. He certainly had a big influence on me. Until I met him, I believed that only dead people from the past in books wrote poetry. Alan was young and from a poor background. Like me, he seemed to have been able to educate himself. Loving words had been a help to him. If he could write poetry then maybe a little hoose daemon could too. So I gave it a bash.

As I said, things didn't really start to change in a big way until the fifties. I've never been a big fan of change – particularly the rapid and sudden kind that throws your entire world upside down. During the twenties and thirties Old Hilda was growing older and Young Hilda was growing up but it happened slowly and I didn't notice it so it didn't worry me. The contents of the dark little house never changed. Occasionally a cup would get broken, a china figurine knocked off a shelf or an old rag rug would become so grubby and tatty and tread worn that it had to be thrown out. And when these inconsequential items disappeared I grieved for them in a small way and felt responsible for their demise being the resident hoose daemon. Likewise I distrusted and kept up an animosity for their replacements. There were certain things – the tea caddies, biscuit barrels, the cheaply framed reproduction of *The Wreck Of The Forfarshire,* Belle's bible, the china fruit dish glazed with the blue painted on ladies, the two wally dogs (one with its nose chipped), wobbly brass candlesticks, the barometer whose mercury had never risen, the model of a Zulu class trawler that poor Willie the Scotsman had made in the shed from driftwood (as well as the wooden box that he carved mermaids and shells on with a nail and which somehow survived the purge of Farquhair), the wedding photograph of Old Hilda and Young

Bert – that I remained so attached to that I thought of them as an extension of myself and I could not bear the prospect of them not being in their time accustomed places let alone not there at all.

The Second World War came and went. It left little mark on life in our little street although most of the young men disappeared to the Army, RAF and particularly the two Navies. Rationing came back for the six years of this War and for a number of years after. But it had little effect on us. The two Hildas were used to living frugally. Neither ate much. When you are poor and used to it you don't miss what you never had. I can remember the bombings of Newcastle and Sunderland. The blokes were all up on the roof. It was 9th April 1941. Seabasstian Haik said, "What's that buzzing noise like sick hornets?" There was a hush for a bit, which was rare among us. We listened and he was right. There was a breeze coming up from the South West. It carried whispers and buzzes, hissing and every now and again a soft crump crump. Then a daemon called Lugworm, who had especially good hearing said, "It's coming from Newcastle way – all's not well down there." In fact, it was Luftflotte 2, dropping 150 tons of explosives and 50,000 incendiary bombs during a five hour attack on the old city. They came back again on the 25th of April and did the same to Sunderland. The reason given for doing this – which we heard from Lord Haw Haw on the wireless, was to incapacitate British industry, in this case to destroy the docks, the ship building and the factories. But it was also to terrify and destroy the courage of the folk by blowing their houses to bits as well as the innocent men, women and children and hoose daemons who lived in them. Sadly, the same thing happened to the German people during the second half of the war when the Allies got the upper hand. Unlike the First War, where it was mainly soldiers who took the terrible brunt of the fighting, as the Second World War unfolded it became clear that everyone was involved whether they liked it or not. Many other horrors would unfold although not everything became clear until the war was over.

Wee Lingy, who had described World War 1 as *a Capitalist War* and who had advocated pacifism ever since then, now changed his mind and described the War against Hitler as 'The only just war ever worth fighting." He claimed that the Nazis were the essence of evil and stood for the opposite of everything that had brought us hoose daemons into being. They had to be destroyed before they destroyed humanity. I did not understand Lingy's words fully at the time but in the light of what I have learned and what has happened since, I realise he was right. I can remember how shocked I was when the war ended and the news and the pictures of the concentration camps where the Nazis imprisoned and murdered the Jews came to light.

A few years after the end of the war there came a chap on the front door. Young Hilda went to answer it and I followed. There stood a pale thin young man in his twenties, shivering. He tried to say something but we could not make it out. He was not local nor in fact British yet he looked somehow familiar. Eventually it was Young Hilda who established that the fellow was in fact French. Young Hilda began to close the door politely but firmly. "No thank you, we have no need of onions today." But the young Frenchman seemed quite animated and rummaging frantically in his greatcoat, produced a torn crumpled letter which he thrust into Hilda's hands.

"Eel – da, oui? Je m'appelle Bertee. Je suis votre frere."

Young Bertee was admitted into *Jonah's Neuk*. I recall that for some time there was considerable consternation and confusion – both Hilda's were talking and shouting at once and I was whizzing excitedly around the ceiling and got entangled in the light fitting. Questions were being fired at Bertee rapidly but he was clearly unable to answer them. He sat there looking bemused and simultaneously nonchalant. He lit up a woodbine and began to smoke. It all seemed a poison d'Avril to him. It took a while to begin to sort things out but eventually some clarity began to emerge. Young Hilda took possession of the letter and read it carefully and slowly, her grey eyes widening with surprise and shortly, tears. Of course, I was squinting over her shoulder as is my custom, greedily taking in as much as I could. "Leave me be, nosey beastie," Young Hilda muttered under her breath. Old Hilda was pacing up and down, her brow furrowed in perplexity.

It turned out that Bertee's crumpled letter of introduction and explanation and farewell had been written by his father – Young Bert, who had not been killed in action at all in March 1917 but who had deserted his post on the Western front. After many mishaps, adventures, strokes of luck and acts of kindness from strangers he had eventually settled in the South of France in a small port near Marseilles where he ended up working on a sardine boat for many years, picking up the local patois in the process. At some point in the thirties he had gotten lucky in some unexplained way. He had invested his savings in a small cafe, married a French wife bigamously who ran the place for him and brought up his second family while he drank red wine and played draughts and had affairs with other French women. Young Bert was never a great letter writer and his literacy skills had not improved very much over the years. There were a lot of grey areas in his narration of events. Much was skipped over or left unexplained but at least he had tried to give an honest account – I gained the impression that Young Bert, now an old man and facing his imminent mortality was trying to make a clean breast of it before it was too late. His letter, which was addressed to Old Hilda, had an arresting opening:

> Dear 'ilda,
>
> This will be a sever shock to you. Yes – it's me, your Bert after all thes years. I have been alive all this time tho not now if you are reading this. You may put the rolling pin away becaws I am pushing up daisies in France by this time if you are reading this and you cannot hit me with it. I am sorry for what I have done

to you and the wee babby. I did not mean it but it seemed to happen anyway. I want you to look after Young Bertee for me. He is not a bad lad but gets imself into trouble and needed to go away for a bit. i ave asked him to give you this letter witch will tell you all about what happened to me . . .

I was unable to read the rest. Tears were flowing down Young Hilda's face as she finished reading the letter and clutched it to her heart. Then she handed it to her Mum. Old Hilda read the thing slowly and with some difficulty, mouthing some of the words silently. Then she crumpled it up and flung it on the fire. "Foolish Man", she muttered then went into the kitchen to fetch Bertee some stottie cake and leek soup. But the crumpled letter did not burst into flame but sat there on a large wet coal, blackening around the edges. Then an updraft suddenly raised it up the chimney. I followed up and caught it, half way up. Re-emerging out the chimney granny I was able to sit on the roof and consider the document in its entirety. Reading the letter, written in Bert's pigeon English and idiosyncratic style which must have taken him a while, possibly days, to complete, I could not help but feel sorry for him in the initial stages. There was one bit that read:

Going to the war seemed a good idear at the time 'ild. Truth to tell it were Billy Mitchell, the mate of *The Canny Man* who first suggested it. Look at us two mugs stuck 'ere Bert, he says. This is us till we're too old for owt but to hang aboot the quay and give the young 'uns sage advice and talk aboot the old days and get in the bloody way. Our lives ain't ever going to change – we'll never earn enough for a part share in a boat, let alone own one. We're missing all the fun. We should sign on and see France and meet some o them foreign lassies before it's over with. Fishing'll still be waiting when we get back and so will Old Hilda. What do you say? And I said "aye" but on the day at Tynemouth Billy chickened out and I signed on the dotted line. Worse thing I ever did. It were 'orrible 'ild. I can't write down how bad. I kent bits of it would be nae picnic but all I could think on was how to get back to Seahouses to you and the wee lass and the boat. Just spare me from this Lord and I'll never complain or girn aboot anything ever again. In the end the Boche machine gunned nearly the whole damned battalion down. There were only a couple of us left standing in the smoke and the mud – all dazed and confused and giddy like. I thought to meself "Sod this for a lark." I turned around and started walking back to our trenches. I'd had enough. On the way I picked up this wounded bloke hanging there groaning away on the wire. I carried him back to the field hospital. Never found what happened to 'im. They said, "lost your medic's armband mate?" so I just nodded. They thought I was ambulance. I kept walking away from the noise of it. It were never anything to do with King or Country or owt like that for me and I weren't ever cut out to be a soldier – couldn't kill anyone if I tried. I used to aim away to the side. I was just bored with being a fisherman. Any roads, I kept walking. Maybe because we lost so many they presumed I was one of them. If they had caught me they would have given me the firing squad but somehow I was lucky. I hid under lorry tarpaulins and in hayricks and ditches and finally got to Paris. There were lots of dossers and tramps there with bits of old uniforms on so I fitted in fine. Started begging with the 'omeless. There was even a bloke with a general's coat – don't know if he stole it or if he were a genuine general wot had had enough. . You've got to believe this next bit 'ild – it were always my intention to get back across the channel and home to Seahouses. But things kept happening that stopped me. I was worried when the war ended that they would still be after me. I might get a long prison sentence and bring shame on the whole family. It was easier to head South, particularly when the winter set in in Paris. Years passed and instead of being easier to come home it got harder – and I knew you wouldn't be best pleased wi' me. I thought it better that you believed I had died a hero's death rather than ran off somewhere in France. Any roads, that's the truth of it 'ild. I'm sad I never made it home to God's ain country as we like to call it, to see you and the lass one more time but these last few days the pair of yous have been much in my thoughts. I've missed yous both. Say a prayer for me and catch you latter,

Yoursly, Bert.

Later that night, in the flickering firelight, I carefully examined the features of Bertee and his elder half – sister Young Hilda. There were certainly many similarities but he did not have eyes that glinted like the sunlight in rockpools. It occurred to me, as he leaned back contentedly with his feet up on the fire guard, arrogantly puffing out Woodbine smoke that he might share his half-sister's gift and be able to see hoose daemons. He could not. even the finest of actors would have evinced some form of facial reaction as I danced an insulting and comical hornpipe almost on the tip of his long Gallic nose. He didn't even blink.

Now *Jonah's Neuk* had a new inhabitant. Bertee might not have the ability to see daemons but he certainly had an eye for the main chance and he proved it many times during his short stay that seemed to last a much longer while. He was indolent, feckless and devious and had perfected all three vices to a fine art. He was also moody and sarcastic, picking up English quickly but only to express himself in a negative way. He also picked up a fair amount of coarse and foul language from the fishermen in no time at all, some of which shocked even Bob Cod when he heard him cursing the landlord outside *The Schooner* who had barred him one night after running up an excessive tab. I understood why his dad's last instruction was for him to be packed off to a foreign country tooth sweet. Otherwise the family cafe business would have gone bankrupt. Bertee spent his waking hours, which thankfully for all concerned were mercifully short, between the pub, the bookies and chatting up the local girls. Getting up sometime in the early afternoon, he would raid old Hilda's tea caddie for cash and head off in the bus to Newcastle, sometimes coming home the worse for wear and sometimes not coming home at all. Sometimes covered in bruises and other times lipstick. And once, for some unaccountable reason, bound up tightly in bandages like *The Mummy* although otherwise unscathed.Young Hilda quickly got the measure of him and made sure that he had no access to her hard worked for earnings but Old Hilda did not seem to be able to refuse him and stoically endured his plundering of her scant resources. She had a soft spot for him and a sense of duty – a bad combination. Bertee was with us for nine months but it seemed a lot longer.

One time I asked Bob Cod a question."Bob," I said, "you seem to be the furthest travelled among all us hoose daemons here – where's the furthest you've been to?"

At this Lingy interrupted, "*says* he's the furthest travelled," he snorted significantly.

Roller Skate interjected soothingly,"Ahem – Bob's what you

might call an empiricist, Tammy. He's not a bookman like me but he likes to – ahem – see proof of things with his own eyes. Lingy here on the other hand is – ahem – more of a theoretician. He seeks for underlying patterns and rules that govern our visible and invisible world."

"Empiricist eh?" said Lingy, "Is that a fancy word for a lying bugger?"

"I'll have none o that from you little Lingy," said Bob, affronted. "One more interruption and Tammy here'll not get to hear the story of how I got to Norway – which incidentally is bloody far away – further than you've ever been any day Lingy. It's almost as far as Fiddlers' Green."

"By Saint Cuthbert's beads !" exclaimed Wullie Whitebait.

"You're too early with that Wullie – that's supposed to come at the end. Now hush up all of you, while I tells me tale . . .

I had always wanted to visit Norroway ever since I saw the Viking blokes plundering Lindisfarne. Big hairy chaps they were with long hair and beards and axes and they made an awful noise – a bit like those fellows I once saw at Newcastle City Hall – what were they calling themselves again- *Uriah Heep*? I was fascinated by them Vikings. Boy – could they drink ale, swear and tell tall tales. They'd cause a fight in an empty house them. When they weren't chopping the heads off the monks they would fight amongst themselves and have wrestling matches and bet on who would be the winner. And when one of them lost all his booty he would pick a fight with the one who won it off him then they would have another wrestling match and so it went on. Very entertaining. Anyway – it was always my ambition to go across the sea to Norway to see what kind of land these terrible creatures came from and to observe their society like."

"That's a lang journey like – over there, especially for a hoose daemon." said Scampy Finnan.

"It is that Scampy – too far by half for me. And that's why it took me over three hundred years to get there. And I never would have but for a lucky chance. One day a ship put in at Seahouses harbour. There had been a bit of a storm and the captain, a canny lad, put in to the harbour to wait the storm out rather than risk running aground on big Harcer. It was from abroad or somewhere like that and it carried a precious cargo – stuff for the King of Scotland. The King of Scotland, like most Kings, liked to treat himself to the very best that money could buy – despite the fact that most of his people lived on cold seaweed and turnip soup. But the King of Scotland was a particularly tight tightwad. Fine silks, jewel encrusted breeks, delicious wine, peacocks feathers, ivory combs for his ladies in waiting, you name it – it was in the hold of that ship. On a whim, I decided to jump on board when the ship set sail again. Scotland was another distant land I had often thought of visiting. The King of Scotland at that time had a palace in Dunfermline. The ship I was on was bound for a small port nearby called Aberdour. We got there without mishap after a couple of days and I disembarked onto dry land and decided to have a ramble about to get me bearings and a feel of this strange Northern land.

I went down to a bit called the Silver Sands and there I did meet with a handsome young man. He was tall and athletic looking and he had blue eyes and a mane of golden hair. He was standing reading a letter and the tears were running down his cheeks. "I'm done for," he sighed, "that old buzzard has stitched me up like a kipper."

And that was exactly what had happened. Young Pat – for that was his name – was reading his own death warrant and that was why he was so upset.

I picked up the story listening into the gossip in the local taverns and pubs. Now it turned out that the King, who was a particularly greedy and materialistic individual, wanted to marry the King of Norroway's daughter, who was named Margaret and was just a young girl. He was after the rich dowry that would be brought back with her and he needed it in a hurry to pay off his many foreign debtors. The more you look into the affairs of humans the more you find out that it's usually all about money, politics or sex. It was the worst of winter and the chances of getting over the grim and gurly North Sea and back in those days without being sunk were around 20%. Basically it was a suicide mission for whoever was picked to skipper the king's ship. That's why Pat was crying his pretty eyes out. You see, he was a well thought of lad. A good skipper and popular with his crew. He always bought his round. But Pat's undoing was his popularity with the ladies. One in particular, the young pretty wife of the king's elderly first minister had been making covetous eyes at him. The First Minister, a cold conniving man, had noticed what was going on but chose to say or do nothing until the right time. Then he picked his moment. He had a quiet word in the king's lug. "Pick him, he's good. He'll bring home the bacon safely." And Pat couldn't refuse. He'd have had his head chopped off by the King's executioner if he had refused.

So there was nothing else to do but make a decent fist of it. They set sail just before Christmas into the teeth of a howling Nor' Easter. There was the crew and a crowd of free loaders – young courtiers who had tagged along on the chance of getting to meet some Scandinavian women. I had decided to jump aboard knowing that it might be my only chance of getting to see Norway. I soon wished I hadn't. The journey over was terrible. I pride myself on my sea legs, even though I don't actually have any real legs, but the roll and swell was something terrible and everyone was sick bar Pat – even the crew. The courtiers stayed down below only surfacing occasionally to vomit over the side. I wrapped myself around the main mast and kept my eyes firmly on the horizon. The amazing thing is that thanks to Pat's brilliant seamanship we actually got there intact – just before the New Year.

At first we were made real welcome and invited into the King's Long Hall, but over the holiday season the courtiers and crew soon wore out their welcome. The King of Scotland had sent over some cheap rubbish as gifts for the Norwegians – tartan nick nacks, fousty haggis and rotgut whisky which were accepted graciously enough. However it soon became apparent that the young Scots courtiers, out for a party, were about to finish off Norway's supplies of beer and wine double quick. They were a real nuisance. They were uncouth and boorish. They insulted the womenfolk. They wound up the men. They scandalised the young ladies by lifting up their kilts at every opportunity. Free from the everyday restraints of their native society they chose to act like stereotypes. They fell into peoples' kail patches and peed in their flower baskets. And they thought they were being a great laugh. The Norwegians didn't think that.

In fact, they couldn't wait to be rid of them. But their atrocious behaviour did speed up the diplomatic process. Any doubts the Norwegian King, Harold Greentooth, may have had concerning sending his young daughter off to a land inhabited by lager louts were quickly waived in consideration of the disastrous effect the Scottish mission was having on the Norwegian treasury – besides, as smiles of polite welcome gave way to snarls of annoyance and frustration it began to look like a major international incident was in the offing. Poor little Margaret was packed off with her maids in waiting. The Scots lairds were hustled aboard Pat's ship, still hungover and bid a fond farewell. See you again folks – but not for a while! maybe three centuries! A large number of kegs of ale were rolled aboard as well as a sweetener. I'm told that the Scots appalling behaviour left such a lasting impression on the Norwegians that to this day Norway remains in the main, a non alcoholic society. And this in the land that spawned the Vikings. Many of the courtiers were still drunk as the ship set sail for home and one was clearly seeing double claiming that he could see the new moon and the old moon at the same time – despite the fact it was mid morning. Soon the party had kicked off again down below and folk were being sick over the side rail and all points windward.

Amazingly, good weather kept up all the way back. The sea was as calm as a millpond. There was a stop over at Shetland for a knees up and another for a ceilidh at Aberdeen. We sailed down the East coast and into the Forth without so much as a lazy ripple or a gentle zephyr. It looked like Pat had pulled it off – he had brought the King of Scotland's bride home along with a dowry hoard of silver and gold and other fine pressies. He would end up Admiral of the Scottish Navy.

Tradition tells of a mighty storm that blew up *half ower, half ower fae Aberdour*. This is not the case. I know because I was bloody there. What really happened was that down below an unfixed beer keg was pushed over by an inebriated oaf. It rolled midships and knocked into a bulwark that caused a spar to spring. The bottom of the ship began to fill up with water, slowly at first. Bit by bit Pat's ship began to list. They were all too drunk to notice. By the time the cabin boy alerted Pat there were leaks springing in other places. Then there was a sproinging noise and a huge inrush of water into the keel of the warped ship of state. Pat ordered his crew to grab piles of expensive silk and clothes that were part of the dowry and stuff them into the gaping holes in the timbers to keep out the sea. But it was pandemonium. The crew were trying to get down below but were met by the drunken lairds trying to escape. Fights broke out and mad eyed with terror, jumpers hurled themselves overboard. Blokes were pushing and shoving and effing and blinding. Freeloaders were stuffing their doublets with whatever they could lay their hands on.

And yet they almost made it. Dry land was in sight. All the ladies had come out in their finery to welcome the new queen. We could see them lined up all pretty like and waving at Aberdour harbour. Then suddenly the boat tipped up stern first. It was all over pretty quickly. Screams of anguish rent the air. Quickly Pat's ship sank. Bubbles. Flotsam. I was hanging on grimly to the crow's nest and was the last to enter the salty water. I leapt into the sea as the mast went under. It was freezing. Most of the crew and passengers went down with the ship and never came up. I never saw Pat. A few sobered souls tried to struggle ashore but the icy cold gripped them and took them down as well. I scrambled on top of a floating beer keg and rode my luck. It finally brought me ashore at a place called Pettycur, a few miles downriver. As I sailed down the Forth on the last beer keg I could hear the wails and lamentations coming from the shore. And that's about it – the story of how I went to Norway and back again – you can say your bit now Wullie."

But Lingly said," If you believe that then you'll believe anything. That's even worse than your story of how you became the cook on the *Marie Celeste*."

Roller said solemnly, "Sadly – ahem – students of Scottish History can point to episodes such as Flodden, Culloden, The Darien Scheme and Ally's Tartan army as evidence of a propensity in the DNA of that benighted nation to snatch defeat from the jaws of victory. This seems to be confirmed by Bob's – ahem – direct experience."

"Yes but Bob," I said, "What did you think of Norway?"

"Pretty boring really. Bit of a disappointment. There were no Vikings. Just farmers and blokes being henpecked by their wives. A very conservative society I would say. I suppose the scenery was ok – if you like your mountains and fiords. But there's only so much. The farms were all on little flat bits at the mouths of the fiords. I think that's how the Vikings started really – they were glad to sail away and create some excitement. Change of beer's as good as a holiday! But them Scotsmen – they should have been barred."

After Bertee was similarly barred from all of the local bookmakers and turf accountants he ran his own highly illegal operation for a while down at the quay. He returned home late one evening when the two Hilda's were abed, grinning like the Cheshire cat. Removing his jacket I saw that he had wrist watches all the way up both of his arms. These had been won from the local fisherlads in lieu of money. Bertee had had a good night, cleaning everyone out. This gave him great confidence in his entrepreneurial abilities. But alas the next night Bertee returned to the house crumpled and limping badly, his face swollen like a rotting pumpkin. Both eyes were loaded with thunder and he was spitting out congealed blood and fragments of teeth. Bertee had had a bad night and had been unable to cover the bets he had lost. The reaction had been swift and his bookies business was now at an end. Bertee was in fact lucky not to have gone in the harbour head first. He had brought excitement and considerable worry to *Jonah's Neuk* after many quiet years but it couldn't last. One morning he was gone and he has not to date returned. He left behind a number of objects that he claimed to have found about the town. Young Hilda was able to return some of these to their original owners but there remained a number of items including a canteen of cutlery, a baleful stuffed badger in a glass case, a monogrammed silk gentleman's dressing gown and an prosthetic left leg that lay around the house until the day that Farquhair Tinkerson had it emptied. The whole episode of Bertee had a powerful effect on Young Hilda – whether negative or positive I cannot say. Shortly after Bertee's departure she finally stopped walking out with Mr. Tom Brocklehurst, the local librarian and widower with whom she had maintained an ambiguous and lukewarm relationship for many years. They had been in the habit of going for a Sunday walk and an ice cream, alternately along the beach and along the golf course besides, of course, meeting on a Tuesday evening in the premises of the Labour club (above the magic shop) of which Mr. Brocklehurst was the secretary. It was as if the exemplars provided by her dad and half – brother had made up Young Hilda's mind that relationships with the untrustworthy male sex were not worth the bother. Young Hilda kept up her membership of the Labour Party though until the coming of the witch Thatcher in the late nineteen seventies when she joined the Socialist Workers Party.

A few weeks after Bertee had gone there was an abrupt rap on the front door. Young Hilda answered. There had been a few such calls already – mainly irate men looking for their money back. Once it was the local Bobby with a notebook full of questions. This time it was the burly Mitchell brothers. They wanted to have a word with Bertee about their cousin Dot. She was in the family way. Had he left a forwarding address?

CHAPTER SEVEN

All Fall Down

Phew! The Blackberries have gone – finally. Whew! That is a long sigh of relief mixed with some considerable joy. Phew! Whew! Yip, yip yaroo! Good riddance and I hope I've seen the back of you for good, you absolute pests. Mind you, they did not slip away quietly or without fuss. That would have been too much to ask. No, there were fights and rows to the bitter end. Mr. Blackberry could not find his adaptor and accused Reginald of taking it and flushing it down the toilet. Reginald accused his brother Ronald of breaking his computer football game by jumping on it and Ronald accused Reginald of stealing and hiding his robotic snake – a foul and invidious thing which in fact now resides in the glove compartment of Farquhair Tinkerson's four wheel – for some reason I am able to master a consul joy stick without too much bother. Mrs. Blackberry was still accusing her husband of being far too soft with Farquhair, even as they were going out the front door and she threatened further letters and phone calls when she got home. "You're far too soft. You should have got more out of him in the way of compensation after all he's put us through this week. Some Marks and Spencers gift vouchers would have been nice. It will be a relief to get back to somewhere civilised. Ugh! – I hate this pokey place. It stinks of kippers," she informed him.

I suppose she knows the price of everything and the value of nothing, as the saying goes. Folk like the Blackberries are incredibly tight when it comes to their money. They do not appear to be badly off compared to many poor souls, some of whom do not even have a roof over their heads. Nevertheless, the Blackberries, despite their propensity for haggling and arguing and their determination to get the best deal for everything from pet gerbils to gymnasium membership subscriptions, never quite seem to be managing their finances well at all. They fritter much of it away on not getting the thing they really need rather than the nearest cheap deal substitute. Likewise they never seem to enjoy the things their wealth is spent on very much. They collect rather than use and they never look after what they have or appreciate how lucky they are. I'm sure both would mock Belle and Old Hilda's habit of keeping their pennies and pounds in the tea caddie below the bed but on the other hand neither of these two were ever ripped off at the interest rates the Blackberries are having to sustain monthly. I know this because I could not get to sleep last night for hearing them row about what came off whose credit card and who had spent what on line this month. I didn't understand the details but I picked up the gist. Unhappy people.

They were already going to be late for the Nobson's dinner party that evening by the time Mrs. Blackberry got home, had a bath and got her new cocktail dress on and Mrs. Blackberry was definitely determined to be there although she seemed to detest the Nobsons considerably and did not have a nice word to say about them. They sounded like slightly better off versions of themselves. Mr. Blackberry was clearly keen also to depart but informed his wife that she would have to attend the Nobson's dinner party on her own as he had work to catch up with. He looked glad to be going back to his world of grubby deals but another row started up at this point nevertheless. And all this before they were even packed up and had fought over who was carrying what out to the car! Maybe I'm getting old and unreasonable but the Blackberries have been the most stressful visitors who have resided at *Jonah's Neuk* yet. Even more stressful than the awful alcoholic English teacher in his fifties who came with his exhausted poor long suffering wife one October weekend to write his novel, have his breakdown and complain incessantly about how no one understood his genius and how his life had been thrown away in the pursuit of meaningless goals. He was hard work him – he was what Lingy would refer to as a moaning git – and his novel, which I read over his shoulder, was the biggest load of self pitying tripe – yet he was still not in the same irksome league as the Blackberries.

But all things must pass and the rain must be followed by the sun – though sometimes it seems there are a good few weeks of torrential downpour before the sun blinks weakly and appears shyly for a brief half hour. Peace descended and I could feel the old place untensing itself. I relaxed and drifted off into memories of days gone by in *Jonah's Neuk* . . .

Doris was a little fat freckled bundle of joy with tousy brown hair and bearing a slight resemblance to Bertee, Dot Mitchell, Old and Young Hilda – though not all simultaneously.

She was clever at school and won the prize every year for being the most able pupil. This was remarkable because no one before in the Mitchell family had shown such academic potential previously and in fact the family had something of a reputation for being rough and ready and what is now referred to as dysfunctional.

Back then they were called various unsavoury names , such as toerags and tinks and minks and various other appellations that connoted their status as ne'er do wells. A good part of Doris' advantage in respect of her precosity lay in the fact that from early on, Young Hilda, perhaps recognising a familial responsibility or maybe just feeling guilty about her half-brother's callous indifference and constant absence, took it upon herself to look out for the toddler who was in need of such beneficial attention and guidance both materially and spiritually. After Old Hilda died suddenly – she dropped down suddenly in the kitchen with a brain haemorrhage – and Young Hilda inherited *Jonah's Neuk,* Doris became a regular visitor and sometimes lodger almost from the time she could first walk. Young Hilda saw to it that she was clothed, fed and generally looked after well. More to the point, she took her education in hand, teaching her her multiplication tables at the kitchen table and showing her how to form letters with a pencil and how to sound out words from a book when she was just a little lass at primary. Later on she bought her text books and encouraged her in many ways – including subsidising her to stay on at school and sit her A levels at a time when Doris came under severe pressure from the Mitchell family to get a job at the checkout in the wondrous new supermarket that the Co op had opened in the town. It was as if Young Hilda was determined that Doris would be given all the opportunities that she was never given herself. Personally I have always believed that environment is much more important than genetics and Young Hilda's input, patience, generosity and kindness finally paid off when Doris became the Dux of the school with a set of qualifications that allowed her an unconditional acceptance to enroll at Durham University to study for an English Literature degree. Again, this did not happen without a struggle and involved determination, persuasion and considerable financial sacrifice on Young Hilda's part. Because Hilda invested in buying books for the purpose of Doris' education and because she insisted that the books be kept at *Jonah's Neuk* due to the fact that if Doris took them home the Mitchell family would sell them, during Young Hilda's time an extensive library grew at *Jonah's Neuk*. When Doris had read them Young Hilda read them after and of course, I read them, perched on Young Hilda's shoulder and thus was able to educate myself.

Doris was part of a fortunate generation in the nineteen sixties who were given an opportunity or rather a window of time to develop themselves, experiment with their lifestyles and at least have a brief period in their lives to have a think about who they were and what they might do in the future without being unduly constrained by the demands of Society to get a job, get themselves into debt and thereafter be straitjacketed into towing the line. This was what was known as education at the time. The concept and the meaning have since changed considerably and it is all now inexorably linked with the notion of vocational training and earning money in some form or other. Back then it was a more personal, individualistic and selfish concept and much the better for it. It was still an elite who were eligible and Doris was fortunate in her timing and sponsorship in this respect. However for a short spell, it was a slightly more egalitarian kind of elite with a few more of the poorest folk allowed into Hogwarts than before or after. A generation whose parents had fought in the war, dug coal in the mine, or forged steel in the factory were happy enough to rough it in drafty slums eating ragout and pasta as long as they had the price of a pint or a smoke – in return they attended the odd mildly interesting lecture while getting on with the main business of experimenting – with each other, the guitar or painting, writing poetry or changing the world for the better or just sitting about with pals talking nonsense. This is an extension of childhood play and all adult humans should be given this opportunity – if you start doing it young enough then the habit never leaves you.

Because I have observed and lived in the company of humans all of my life while at the same time being in isolation from them due to the fact that they cannot see me or communicate with me, it is perhaps inevitable that I have mixed feelings about them. They can be quite fascinating to observe and they are all different yet very much alike. I have also observed the relationship between them and dogs. There are some dogs who think of humans as being dogs as well – just different dogs that walk on two legs and are a bit smarter. Being pack animals, they acquiesce to these big human dogs and obey them and give them due deference – albeit trying it on a bit every now and then. On the other hand, there are some dogs who, because they have lived around humans so much, think of themselves as not dogs at all but humans – presumably they see their masters as smarter versions of their own human selves and obey them and give them due deference therefore. What's the difference? I don't know. But cats are different. The reason I say all this is because there are times when I almost think of myself as being human but there are other times when I can see them quite objectively, just as a dolphin sees a shark or a mongoose a cobra. But I can never bring myself to be consistent about it. It can be very frustrating to watch anything continually making mistakes like a lobster entering the same creel for some tasty bait or a seagull taking a bath in an oil slick but I'm pretty sure, even if they could understand me, that I would get little thanks for intervening in their affairs or giving advice. And after all, who am I to give anyone advice?

As the other hoose daemons have slipped away I've became more unsure of myself. When they were around I had sounding boards to bounce ideas off and voice my doubts to. A little communication every day is necessary and being on your own all the time can make you a bit depressed and seeing the downside of everything. Many years ago I asked Roller Skate about *Fiddler's Green* – what it was and where it was. It was after Pincer Crab failed to turn up for the rooftop parliament and we were all feeling sad and fed up and missing him.

"Ahem – a very good question Young Tammy Norrie – *Fiddler's*

Green is a legendary imagined afterlife, where there is perpetual mirth, a fiddle that never stops playing, and dancers who never tire. Its origins are obscure, although some point to the Greek myth of the "Elysian Fields" as a potential inspiration. It has – ahem – related variants known, to name but a few, as *The Land of Cockagne* and *Tir Na Nog*. The Vikings, who Bob Cod knew well, called it *Valhalla* and in Arthurian legend it is *Avalon* the place where Arthur sleeps until the hour of Albion's need. For sailors and all those who have – ahem – an umbilical link to the sea it is known as *Fiddler's Green*. One sailor's tale published in 1832 speaks of Fiddler's Green as being – ahem – "nine miles beyond the dwelling of his Satanic majesty". In maritime folklore it is a kind of afterlife for sailors who have served at least fifty years at sea,where there is free rum and tobacco in abundance and where no work or subservience to an officer/boss class is required."

At this Lingy broke in – "Aye, that's right. Geordie Orwell called it *The Big Rock Candy Mountain* in his book *Animal Farm*. And it's a right load of bollocks enaw."

"I'm not sure that I quite understand your drift Lingy?" said Roller Skate.

"I don't believe in it," said Lingy flatly, "It's a human notion we've picked up. And we should knaw better. There's nae such place if you diven't mind me saying. There's nae *Fiddler's Green* anymair than there's a Peter Pan and Neverland. The day I see *Fiddler's Green's* the day Newcastle United'll win the Premier League and nae mistake, me bonny lads."

Lingy's words provoked an angry response from the other hoose daemons who were not impressed by his cynicism. They shouted and hooted him down. "By Saint Cuthbert's Beads!" exclaimed Wullie Whitebait.

Yet Lingy stuck to his guns. He enjoyed winding them up. "The humans are first class at feeding their bairns a right load of cod's roe with pie and peas thrown in – think of all the tall tales they tell them, from Jemima Puddle-Duck to Bilbo Baggins, from little people behind the skirting boards to talking beavers and lions living inside bloody wardrobes. Neither wonder their bairns are right screwed up and flummoxed. And they go on, secretly believing it all when they grow up. I suppose that life is so miserable for most of the poor sods that they have to invent fabulous stories to make it all seem more interesting and make them feel there's a better place later on, further up the road. Nae worries eh?Mouldy bread today but jam the morrow, me bonny lads. And you stupid lot are going down the same road with your *Fiddler's Green*."

"Yes – but where exactly is it and how do you get there?" I asked. Sandy Eilden knew the answer.

"It finds you," he intoned solemnly in sepulchrous tones. "I've heard it said that there's a big black ship sails right into the harbour in the dead of night. You'll know it's there because it will sail into your dreams as well. It's like a big Viking boat with a dragon prow that stands tall out of the water like a sea serpent. It is crewed and rowed by ghostly daemons who led bad lives. There fate is to ferry others to *Fiddler's Green* but never go there themselves. And the dark ship won't go away until you go down to the harbour and climb aboard. It's best not to delay or run away because it's no use. Time stands still when it is anchored in the harbour. The stars don't move and the moon doesn't roll. The sea lies still and the town sleeps. Best go down to the quay and get on board. You have to go alone. No time for goodbyes. Then it sails. It sails out far at a great speed, far beyond the humps and bumps and submerged coils of the great worm we call the earth, beyond time and space itself to the place in the ocean where the stars drop from the sky at the end of night and the coming of day. There is a fleet of dragon prows biding there waiting. Some are there to catch the falling stars and fetch them home to the place where they arise from again at twilight. But your ship is there to take you to *Fiddler's Green*. You may be waiting out there on the deep for a while but at some point the great dragon prow will dip and the entire ship will submerge beneath the waves. It now sails under the ocean, not on it because the surface of the ocean is a portal or gateway between two worlds. I have heard it said that the journey might take long and be a terrifying one or it may be short and peaceful and without mishap and the great sea monsters will allow you free passage – it all depends on the kind of life you have led and the honour you have accrued. Eventually your hope is always that the ship will resurface at *Fiddler's Green,* which is an island in the far West where the great sun ship that all life depends on harbours and weighs anchor at the end of each day. Well, that's the way I heard it any road – so you can believe it if you want or not. The thing is – you're not going to see that boat until your time comes around and you are called."

"By Saint Cuthbert's beads!" exclaimed Wullie Whitebait.

"Bollocks Man!" spat Lingy.

All this was said many years ago. Now Bob Cod, Lang Lamphray, Sandy Eilden, Harry Haddock, Wullie Whitebait, Scampy Finnan, Roller Skate, Crabby Pincer, Bedey Monkfish and Seabasstian Haik have all gone to *Fiddler's Green*. Lingy's not here either so I wonder where he is? Maybe if you don't believe they don't let you in. But I hope he made it there as well, if only to renew his faith in a Newcastle United title win one day. He was right about one thing though – I can see through the attic skylight that the strange Goth couple with the wall wide TV screen are watching *Harry Potter*. They've had a film channel on all day. Earlier on it was *Toy Story* followed by *Star Wars* followed by a documentary about *the Royal Family*. You shouldn't fill your children's heads with too much nonsense. It does them harm. Mind you, there's a house further down the road that has the Science Channel on. Must be teachers. I looked in and tuned in for a few minutes to see what their tele had to say for itself. It was Stephen Hawking going on about something called the Big Bang that can be backed up with mathematical equations so therefore is truth rather than fiction – he seems to have forgotten that numbers didn't exist until humans invented them – and that was a long time after his big bang. Another kind of fairy tale . . .

For a while Doris believed she was living in a fairy tale. She took to life at Durham University like a duck to water and a seal to a seaweedy rock. Once she got over her initial working class inferiority complex and natural shyness, realising that she was every bit as clever as the posh students with the plummy Southern accents, she started to really enjoy the English Literature course. Young Hilda had instilled in her a love of books so she had already read many of the authors if not the individual books that she was to study. Doris enjoyed the tutorials, particularly when she was allowed to express her own opinions and theories. She did not understand all the poets, dramatists and novelists that came tumbling suddenly into her consciousness but she worked hard and got the best of it. She found Wordsworth self obsessed, Poe trivial but Shakespeare and Chaucer she loved. Having grown up in a family with little money her grant at that time seemed generous enough and perfectly adequate. She took on a part time job as a barmaid and was even able to send a little money home for the Mitchell family, who were mainly on the dole at this point, to waste on booze, fags and bingo – but she did not grudge them it because she realised that she had been given a fantastic opportunity to escape the kind of life they were destined to live out.

Being a bright and canny lass she started to figure out how the system operated. For one thing she discovered that some of the posh kids with the plummy accents were not from the South at all. Some were from middle class families in the North who had been packed off to public schools like Fettes and Heriots' in Edinburgh. Some were from poor backgrounds just like herself but had quickly adopted and adapted their accents to distance themselves from their roots. You could never be sure when you were talking to someone over a coffee in the refectory or having a half pint of cider in the Union who they really were. At the end of a lecture the member of staff would direct the class to a particular edition of a textbook that must be bought. If it was say, Milton's *Paradise Lost* it would turn out that the particular edition had been edited by the member of staff who had recommended it. No other edition was deemed acceptable. In tutorials the tutor would often play the devil's advocate role – in these situations you had to be careful. Originality of thought and opinion was not always the best policy and might lead to either a curt dismissal or far worse, a lengthy and toe curling dissection of your shaky argument. In this case the student had fallen into a carefully prepared trap designed to show how clever the tutor was by comparison. In order to achieve this the tutor would often retain or hold back certain information in order to maintain an advantage. Some of the more ambitious students seeking firsts were happy enough to play this game but Doris knew instinctively it was not for her. She had neither the confidence nor the temperament to push herself to the fore – she was happy enough to keep her head down and avoid becoming an easy target. A 2:1 at the end of it all was her ceiling. Doris was contented enough with where she was.

But there was something else – Doris had a boyfriend. A steady boyfriend who she had met at the Fresher's Ball. He was a second year student. He was one of the public school boys from Fettes and his name was Farquhair Tinkerson. As the Christmas holidays approached Doris was in a turmoil of excitement and confusion and doubt. She desperately wanted to bring Farquhair home to Seahouses to show him off to the family but she was terrified that they might show her up and embarrass her or that even her ruffian cousins would rough him up. In the end Doris settled for a compromise . . .

A brief visit – in fact it lasted little more than ten minutes – to meet her family then round to *Jonah's Neuk* for afternoon tea with Young Hilda was the final plan. Doris had already told Farquhair all about this lovely lady and what a benefactress and second mother she had been to her and I'm sure that even at that early stage Farquhair was figuring out how to con money from this strange species that he had never previously encountered in his short life – a genuinely giving and generous soul. For Farquhair had been brought up as the runt of a litter of snobs. Born into a well to do Borders family who traced their lineage back to Robert The Bruce, his father had been Sheriff of the County and his mother was a biographer of Sir Walter Scott. Farquhair's elder brother had studied Law at St. Andrews before joining a prestigious Edinburgh Law firm as a partner and his elder sister was married to a Conservative MP who lived in a fortified house in rural Perthshire. The damage had been done to Farquhair at an early age – brought up in a house of ice, a sliver of it had entered his heart and there was no undoing that terrible wound. A disappointment to all, almost from the moment of his birth (and well he knew it and had been reminded of it), he had been too thick to study law like his brother and his father had wanted him to join the army. It hadn't worked out due to merciless bullying and now he was doing a Business Degree. In truth, he was well suited to it because the acquisition of money was all that Farquhair was interested in. So he turned up at *Jonah's Neuk* with Doris giggling on his arm in her beehive and mini skirt, him in his green waxed jacket with his round pink face and numerous even teeth and untrendy neat army haircut, his piggy eyes sizing up everything round about him.

I never liked him from the minute I first saw him and when Young Hilda, all in a fluster and babbling a complete load of nonsense, dottered through to the kitchen to fix up sandwiches and cakes and tea, he immediately started pulling faces and mimicking her. He picked up some of the cheap ornaments that lay on the mantlepiece and looking at their bottoms sneered at them. Then he pretended he was going to chuck them in the fireplace. I was horrified. I was even more horrified with Doris' reaction. I waited on her to give a him a good slap across the lugs or at least to tell him off. But she only giggled nervously and whispered,"Farquhair, stop being silly." It was at this point that I decided I'd had enough. I decided to head out for the day and not return until they had gone. So I went up the coast to Lindisfarne where I met Alan on the beach.

It was my assumption all along that the relationship between Farquhair and Doris was never meant to last – she was not his type. It would be easy to say that he turned her towards his own cold ways but the truth was that Doris had hooked him and was equally determined not to let go of her trophy. In order to change her life on a permanent basis she had to make sacrifices. In doing so she lost much and gained Farquhair. In some ways Farquhair's self confidence had been so eroded by his horrible family that he needed a compliant working class woman to reinforce his precarious self esteem so that he could strut around like a little peacock. Or maybe he married Doris just to spite them. Who knows? In capturing Farquhair Doris proved adroit. First the news filtered back that they had become engaged and then one day an invitation arrived at *Jonah's Neuk* for Young Hilda to attend their wedding. And then they were married. Doris never completed her degree. By the time she should have the first baby had arrived. Doris succeeded in changing her life on a permanent basis. Young Hilda was heartbroken but like her mother she was not one to say much. Who could she tell or complain to?

And the years passed and Young Hilda grew old. These were quiet happy years at *Jonah's Neuk* and I paid little attention to what was going on in the outside world. Apart from the cataracts that caused her to lose her vision and stop her from reading her beloved books, Young Hilda enjoyed excellent health. Her mind was as sharp as ever and her body never faltered or let her down. She was an active old lady even though she could hardly see. She would be away up the street to the shops in the morning with her two sticks clacking on the pavement, going at a pace that I could barely keep up with. We saw Doris rarely and she never brought Farquhair along, which was fine with everyone. She would arrive with the babies twice a year – when it was Young Hilda's birthday and just after Christmas. Young Hilda loved these days and I swear that she seemed to lose twenty years when a visit from Doris and the bairns was imminent. Farquhair had graduated and gone into the property business. They were doing well. Moving up in the world. Every time they came it seemed they had moved house. It went bedsit – flat – semi detached – bungalow – detached stone built property – detached stone built property with extensive garden. And then very quickly as it seemed to me one day it was just Doris who came for her three bairns had grown old enough to be sent away to boarding school. Doris seemed quite lost.

I associate these years at *Jonah's Neuk* with a sense of peace and contentment. There was only me and Young Hilda and Nicey in the old house. It was quiet and the routine seldom changed. Young Hilda spoke to me quite a lot. Sometimes she would just be repeating local gossip she had heard and other times she would make observations about politics and books and life in general. As her sight deteriorated she got into the habit of listening to the radio a lot – she had it on quietly in a corner of the kitchen and she would listen to the news broadcasts, plays and literary reviews. Although everything was harmonious in *Jonah's Neuk* itself this was the time of Margaret Thatcher, a kind of witch who wanted to turn the North of Britain into a wasteland of dispirited slaves, rather in the fashion of the Snow Queen in Narnia. Young Hilda detested her and so did I. Word of her ill doings was always on the radio news broadcasts. She sowed disharmony and unhappiness everywhere, whether it was attacking the miners and their families and children, denying the primary children their milk, attacking our partners in European countries or going to war in the Falkland Islands and Northern Ireland. She was no better than a criminal yet to this day there are many who defend her. Farquhair was a huge admirer of hers as was one of Farquhair's old school pals – a young politician called Tony Blair who came with his wife to Farquhair and Doris for dinner parties. Eventually Thatcher had her day as they all do – even the worst. But by then she had caused much damage, particularly to the communities of working people in the North. Thatcher hated the idea of there being a Society – particularly a Society that showed care and compassion for the poorest and the worse off. During her time people were encouraged to become greedy and selfish and materialistic and started caring less about their neighbours and families. In such a situation where there are few jobs or industries the young are the hardest hit. Some leave and become economic refugees, some become involved in crime and others just give up hope. In Scotland, where the people had long held different views and had had enough of Thatcher, many of the folk decided it would be a good idea to leave the United Kingdom all together rather than be ruled from London by such a tyrant. Young Hilda often said that if she had been born in Scotland she would have done the same. She looked forward to the refounding of Bernicia – the ancient kingdom of Northumbria in the days before England and Scotland.

It was an intimation of things to come when Young Hilda finally had to go into hospital to have her eyes operated upon. She was away for weeks and it was the first time that it had just been myself and Nicey. The house seemed empty and big and cold. In all my time there had always been a strong woman guiding the helm of the ark. I shivered when I thought about the future. Meanwhile the brothers were beginning to slip away. The well loved faces who sat on the roofs among the smoking chimneys were starting to vanish. The ranks of the parliament were growing thinner. One of the last questions I asked Roller Skate was about sea serpents.

"Tell me about sea serpents, Roller," I asked. There were only the two of us sitting on the roof of the Old Smokery on a cold windy day.

"Why do you ask, young Thomas?" asked the old daemon, his glasses slipping down his fishy nose.

"Well, they seem to crop up from time to time. I thought I saw one today rising up out of the sea – but when I got closer it was a kite. A marvelous multi – coloured kite like a flying dragon. I mean – are they real? And if so where might they be found? I've never seen what I really look like myself – but I have this feeling – an instinct if you like – that I'm a bit . . . how could you put it? Serpentine? Only small."

"Ahem – indeed so Tammy. When you first appeared among us you were very tiny indeed. You reminded the rest of the daemon blokes of those little sand eels that the puffins fill their beaks with. They have little reverse teeth you know, so that they don't lose them when they carry them back to feed their young? Ahem – anyway, the name Sandy Eilden had already been taken so the parliament decided to name you after a bird instead. There was much debate and discussion. Bob Cod believed that it broke with tradition and would bring bad luck but Lingy convinced everyone that it was time for a change – ahem – so Tammy Norrie it was and I must say it suits you well."

"So who named you Roller Skate?" I ventured.

"A very old and venerable hoose daemon who even predated the Vikings and the monks. His name was Saithe. He named me Skate – the appellation *Roller* is – ahem, an informal nickname added at a later date by the blokes. Saithe was named by Scattan who was in turn, named by Stanelock. Stanelock and his human clan came to Britain from Northern Europe. They walked dry shod from what is now called the Lowlands. He claimed to have witnessed the great Tsunami wave that came from Norway that created the English Channel and made Britain an island rather than a peninsula. It came and went in a matter of seconds he said. Changed everything – especially the way people thought for ever after. In the old days hoose daemons lived long.

Ahem – but to get back to your question Tammy. A sea serpent or sea dragon is a type of sea monster, either wholly or partly serpentine.

Sightings of sea serpents have been reported for hundreds of years, and continue to be claimed today. Cryptozoologists have identified more than 1,200 purported sea serpent sightings. It is currently believed that the sightings can be best explained as known animals such as oarfish, whales, or sharks (in particular, the frilled shark) Some cryptozoologists have suggested that the sea serpents are relict plesiosaurs, mosasaurs or other Mesozoic marine reptiles, an idea often associated with lake monsters such as the Loch Ness Monster .

In Norse Mythology *Jormungandr* or *Midagarthsormr* was a sea serpent so long that it encircled the entire world, *Midgard* Some stories report of sailors mistaking its back for a chain of islands. Sea serpents also appear frequently in later Scandinavian folklore, particularly in that of Norway.

In 1028 AD,Saint Olaf is said to have killed a sea serpent in Valldal, Norway, throwing its body onto the mountain Syltefjellet. Marks on the mountain are associated with the legend In Swedish ecclesiastic writer's Olaus Magnus's *Carta Marina* many marine monsters of varied form, including an immense sea serpent, appear.

Hans Egede, the national saint of Greenland gives an 18th century description of a sea serpent. On 6th July 1734, his ship sailed past the coast of Greenland when suddenly those on board saw a most terrible creature, resembling nothing they saw before. The monster lifted its head so high that it seemed to be higher than the crow's nest on the mainmast The head was small and the body short and wrinkled. The unknown creature was using giant fins which propelled it through the water. Later the sailors saw its tail as well. The monster was longer than our whole ship", wrote Egede.

Sea serpent sightings on the coast of New England, are documented beginning in 1638. An incident in August 1817 spawned a rather silly mix-up when a committee of the New England Linnaean Society went so far as to give a deformed terrestrial snake the name *Scoliophis atlanticus*, believing it was the juvenile form of a sea serpent that had recently been reported in Gloucester Harbor. The Gloucester Harbor serpent was claimed to have been seen by hundreds of New England residents, including the crews of four whaling boats that reportedly sought out the serpent in the harbor. Rife with political undertones, the serpent was known in the harbor region as *Embargo*. Sworn statements made before a local Justice of the Peace and first published in 1818 were never recanted.After the Linnaean Society's misidentification was discovered, it was frequently cited by debunkers as evidence that the creature did not exist.

A particularly famous sea serpent sighting was made by the men and officers of *HMS Daedalus* in August 1848 during a voyage to Saint Helena in the South atlantic ; the creature they saw, some 60 feet (18 m) long, held a peculiar maned head above the water. The sighting caused quite a stir in the London papers, and Sir Richard Owen the famous English biologist , proclaimed the beast an elephant seal Other explanations for the sighting proposed that it was actually an upside-down canoe, or a posing giant squid.

Another sighting took place in 1905 off the coast of Brazil. The crew of the *Valhalla* and two naturalists, Michael J. Nicoll and EGB Meade-Waldo , saw a long-necked, turtle headed creature, with a large dorsal fin. Based on its dorsal fin and the shape of its head, some have suggested that the animal was some sort of marine mammal. A skeptical suggestion is that the sighting was of a posing giant squid , but this is hard to accept given that squids do not swim with their fins or arms protruding from the water.

On April 25, 1977, a Japanese trawler , sailing east of Christchurch, New Zealand, caught a strange, unknown creature in the trawl. Photographs and tissue specimens were taken. While initially identified as a prehistoric plesiosaur , analysis later indicated that the body was the carcass of a basking shark.

And that is about everything I know on the subject of sea serpents, young Norrie. Ahem – I suppose, in a nutshell, it all depends on whether you have faith in their existence. Lots of sailors do. If you believe then they can be found everywhere and anywhere. Even in our local harbour here at Seahouses. If you don't believe then you'll probably never see one."

I thought about those monks at Lindisfarne, looking up from their toil, tending their gardens and mending their nets, looking up to see the dragon prows looming and bearing down on them, hearing the terrible cries emit from the dragon throats. I bet they believed in sea serpents at that moment.

Thanks Roller Skate.

"You're welcome young Norbert. Ahem – it's bloody freezing on this roof. I think I'll take myself indoors. I'm feeling my age and the cold."

When young Hilda got home from hospital I rejoiced. The operation had been a great success and she was able to see better. Things went back to normal and the old routine trundled on again. I was happy again. Before I knew it another decade had passed. But I was forgetting something important. It was not so much that Young Hilda was getting very old for a human – as she approached her hundredth year she was still as bright as a baby otter, still reading *the Morning Star* and still getting out and even managing to get up the stairs. She believed in homeopathic medicines and practised yoga and meditation. When she received her telegram from Buckingham Palace she burnt it in the fireplace with great relish saying 'She may be Her Royal Highness to you and the rest of the crawlers, Beastie, but she's plain Mrs. Windsor to me!" No – what I was forgetting was that things always change. Especially when things are going fine. It's the law. One icy morning in November Young Hilda slipped out the back. She had fallen and broken her hip.

I heard her cursing and flew out the back door. Yet there was nothing I could do. Luckily the postman her cries and popped his head round the back. He had his mobile phone out in a second and stayed with Young Hilda till the ambulance came. All this time I was with her, talking to her but she couldn't hear me. She seemed to have gone into some kind of shock and she seemed disorientated as if she did not know were she was in time or place. She spoke about Bertee, her Dad, and her Mum as if they were still around and the years had not rolled on. I was frantic with worry and did not know what to do. If any of the other hoose daemons had been around I would have gone to them but I was the last. Utterly isolated. Eventually the ambulance rolled up in the close and the paramedics came. The postman explained what had happened to them. No neighbours came out for there were none. It was not like the old days anymore. All the houses in the street with a couple of exceptions had been turned into holiday homes. The owners of the occupied houses had driven away to work early that morning. As they put her on to the stretcher gingerly, at last Young Hilda seemed to come back. Her eyes that had always been like rock pools with the sun glinting on them sparkled one more time. "Look after the old place for me, Beastie, I'll be back soon enough." she whispered. She was in a lot of pain. I was screaming at the paramedics, "Where are you taking her to? What is the name of the hospital?" They never responded. There is a book that was a great favourite of Hilda's called *Animal Farm*. She used to read it aloud and I presumed that it was for me that she did. There is a sad bit near the end where the horse Boxer, who is sick, is taken away in a horse box. The deceitful pigs say to the other animals that he is going to receive medical treatment but the sign on the van reveals that he is being sent to the knacker's yard to be slaughtered. His good friend Benjamin the donkey who can read very well, understands in an instant what is going on and frantic with worry and dread he chases down the road after the van. He is unable to keep up with it. He loses his friend. That was what happened to me that day. I had to give up four miles outside Seahouses as the ambulance disappeared over the horizon headed in the direction of Morpeth or Newcastle. I could not keep up no matter how hard I willed myself on. The flashing blue light and the screaming siren kept on getting further away from me. And yet as I collapsed exhausted by the roadside verge, rationality was already kicking in. A voice inside me was telling me, "Be calm. It will be all right. Hilda will return to *Jonah's Neuk* – it will be like what happened before when she went to hospital to have her eyes sorted. Your job is to go back and look after the place until it is time for her to return." And so I did. I returned slowly to *Jonah's Neuk*.

When I got back the book Young Hilda had been reading was lying open on the arm rest of her reading chair beside her reading glasses. It was Bede's *Ecclesiastical History Of The English People*. It lay open at that same page for many months and I was to read it often thereafter and reflect: *The present life of man upon the Earth o king, seems to me in comparison with that time which is unknown to us, like a swift flight of a sparrow through the house wherein you sit at supper in winter, with your eldermen and thains while the fire blazes in the midst, and the hall is warmed, but the wintry storms of the rain or snow are raging abroad. The sparrow,flying in at one door and immediately out the other , whilst he is within , is safe from the wintry tempest; but after a short space of fair weather, he immediately vanishes out of your sight, passing from winter into winter again. So this life of man appears for a little while, but of what is to follow or what went before we know nothing at all.*

With young Hilda away in hospital somewhere for at least a few weeks I presumed that it would be like the previous time. Just myself and Nicey rattling about in the old house. I was wrong about this. When I woke up in the attic space the next morning cuddling Nicey I could hear someone walking about downstairs. Still half asleep I stumbled down the chimney to see what was happening. To my surprise I saw that Farquhair had let himself in. I knew that Doris kept an emergency spare key so maybe I shouldn't have been so taken aback. Farquhair had a little black moleskin notebook and a pencil. He appeared to be making an inventory of the house's contents. He found Young Hilda's purse and helped himself to her pension. He emptied drawers and cupboards, looking out bankbooks and insurance documents. He also had an electronic measuring device. As he went from room he used this device and noted down various figures. I hadn't a clue what he was up to. I was unimaginably frazzled at this point. All I really wanted was to know how Young Hilda was and where she was. If she was in a hospital not too far away I might even attempt a visit. I bellowed and pleaded with him but of course it was no use. It was not his fault that he couldn't hear me but the desecration of the house and Hilda's things was – when he did this I flew at him in frustration and tried to pound him and trip him up. The more I tried the less effective I seemed to be. I think at one stage he became dimly aware of something oppressing him but he was so intent upon his nefarious business – his little piggy eyes had become even smaller and shone with excitement and money lust as he went about it – that he probably thought that the stuffy atmosphere of the house had brought on a headache. It was a relief when he finally left after a three hour root and branch search of Young Hilda's house. He took not only all the money he could find, including the contents of the old cracked brown teapot, the tea caddy and her purse's contents. Young Hilda, like Old Hilda and Belle before her did not believe in banks. She held that usury was one of the greatest sins and always paid in cash or went without. She said she was with the Muslims on that one. Young Hilda's main stash, little that it amounted to, was hidden under the carpet of the seventh stair tread from the bottom. Farquhair did not find this. But I knew he eventually would. He would be back. Meanwhile all I could do was to hang around and stew, waiting to hear news about Young Hilda. I went up the street, listened to conversations on pavements and pubs – nothing. Eventually in the Smokery I overheard the shopgirl tell a woman buying crabs that the old lady along the way had taken poorly and fallen. I could not make out the name of the hospital. "Mark my words – she'll not be back. Not at her age. We won't see her again. These places are full of bugs – you're far safer at home." Exactly what I didn't want to hear.

The next time Farquhair showed up Doris was with him. This was after an anxious fretful week for me. I was torn between wanting to kick them both out the door while desperately wanting to hear what they had to say.

It was difficult to eavesdrop because they were talking like conspirators in whispers. Like two gleeful naughty children. It was at this point that I realised that all those years living with Farquhair had changed Doris – she had become a very slightly less greedy and materialistic version of him.

"Are you sure it will be for the best?" Doris asked.

"Of course, miles better . . ." purred Farquhair, "it's the best thing all round for everybody. This place is too large for someone that age. She'll be looked after properly at the home. I've looked into it and I've chosen a first class place – simply the best. De Lux in fact. If she falls again there'll be someone on hand. Medical care, great food, company, games of bingo, tele, whatever it is that these old people do . . . she'll love it. But the thing is, the thing you have to get through to her is – she has to sign over this place to us. Tell her otherwise the state will have it all. I mean, it's only fair. We can't afford to pay for her bed and board. She's lucky we're taking an interest. Many old people aren't so lucky. So make sure you convince her that it's the only solution. Staying in this dump isn't viable for her at all."

"She can be very stubborn when she's a mind to be," said Doris doubtfully.

"You can do it, old gel. Besides , this fall has knocked some of the pride out of her. Just remember, we *need* this place. Things have been rocky over the last few years and there's no sign of it picking up. This might make all the difference. Even if the holiday home idea doesn't work out long term I can always sell it to pay off some of the overdraft. Lay it on thick to her. Tell her we're going to modernise the place so that kiddies can come and have good holidays. The rent will pay for her stay in the old folk's home. And make sure she signs on the dotted line – you're good with the old bat. Now let's get started – there's work to be done. All this junk will need to be cleared. I'll hire a skip. If it's worthless crap stick a red dot on it. If it looks like we might get a few quid for it, stick a yellow dot on it. Sadly, it looks like it'll be mainly red. If all goes to plan I'll be back here on Tuesday with the builder to price the conversion."

When they had gone I considered what I had to do. I was faced with an enormous challenge. Under the stair carpet – seven up – was the loose stair tread under which lay most of Young Hilda's meagre savings stuffed between the underlay and the stair carpet itself carpet . A bundle of notes were wrapped round with a rubber band. Pretty soon that carpet would be ripped up. If Farquhair didn't find it first it would be quickly trousered by a fat arsed workman. I could not let this happen. But what could I do? I had hardly any physical strength, no limbs to speak of, negligible influence in the corporeal world. I had the weekend and the Monday to move it to safety. I went to sleep thinking up how this might be done.

It took the whole of Saturday just to move the burdensome bundle of cash from out under the stair carpet. I crawled and pushed myself between the two layers and began to head butt the bundle. It was hot and exhausting and at first it never budged. I got quite a headache. It was stuffy and dirty. I felt like a coal miner underground. Infinitesimally it started to shift. A quarter of an inch after an hour. I was at it all day and fell asleep that night, dead done. I got it out from under the carpet finally the next morning. The rubber band was perished. I gnawed on it and it snapped. A day and a bit to move a bundle of cash a foot. This wasn't going to work. What could I do. Wriggling about in the dust under the carpet had done nothing for my sinuses. I sneezed. The top note on the bundle rose up a few inches. I sneezed again. This time it moved forward a few feet down the stairs. I began to blow the note along the floor. I continued blowing, starting to master how to control the direction. I blew it into the living room. Then I blew it into the cold empty grate. Then I blew it up the chimney, following it up. Blowing the twenty pound note in the cool updraft, balancing it on my nose like a performing circus seal, until I reached the little recess in the chimney bricks, two thirds way up. There I stashed the note.

Have you heard of blowing a pile of cash? Well, that was what I did, literally, that whole weekend. I have never been so tired. It takes a lot of breath and will power. But spurring me on was the thought that every banknote note I managed to blow, spit, sneeze and splutter up the chimney was one banknote that Farquhair wasn't going to lay his greedy mits on. I nearly managed the lot. I was blowing the last fiver somewhat feebly through the hall when the key turned in the lock and Farquhair strode in with the builder.

"Look!" said the builder, "there's a five pound note on the floor. Good place this, innit, eh?"

"I'll take that, thank you," said Farquhair, "Now, here are your instructions. We're having to put things on hold for a bit. The old dear is proving to be more stubborn than I thought. so we can't go ahead immediately. If you ask me, I think she's gone totally doolally. Doris says she became quite agitated when she spoke to her and started waffling on about a *beastie* she thinks lives here. I'm going to speak to a Doctor I know who will help me get her certified as one sandwich short of a picnic. That simplifies matters. After that, we can do what we like. We're her executors now, Doris persuaded her. Now – I'm going to tell you what alterations I want done so you can start whenever I give you the word. Mind now, it'll just be for some plebs to stay for a few days so no point using anything expensive – so don't try to con me with your estimate or I'll try someone else. They're probably used to keeping coal in their baths – ha – ha! Bit like Doris's dreadful family."

Young Hilda died within a few weeks of being admitted into the old folk's home. I heard the news from a conversation between the two builders who came to turn the house into a holiday home. "I 'ear the old lady died in the 'ome . . ."

"Yeah – That's why Mr. Greedyguts was looking so bleedin chirpy this morning. This place is 'is now – it's in 'is wife's name but it belongs to 'im, ipso facto like. 'ere – did you see who Spurs 'ave signed?"

I had been expecting the worse but when I heard this it made me feel as low and sad and empty as I ever have been – there was a kind of numbness and shock as well. I couldn't quite believe it even though I knew it to be true. I was in the house but my mind was somewhere else at the same time – some quiet, desolate cold place. I bolted up the chimney and didn't come down for many days. All around me there was hammering, banging, scraping, ripping, tearing and rending. There was shouting and dust but none of it made any difference – I stayed put in the chimney. The house itself shook as if an earthquake tremor had rippled beneath it – it was a lorry rumbling through the close bringing a skip. Then the house was emptied. A van came and all the things with yellow dots were loaded on to it. Things going back to before Belle's time which I had known all my conscious life. Then the red dot stuff was lifted and carted out on to the skip. I could hear it happening. At some point the two men left and the house lay dark and cold and empty. I fell into a restless sleep, half willing that a dark ship should sail into my restive dreams to carry me away out under the night star harvest. It never came.

For the next few days this was the way of it. I stayed well out of the way while the unbearable alterations took place in *Jonah's Neuk*. It was the two builders who carried out most of the devilish work. Occasionally a plumber or electrician or plasterer would turn up. Sometimes Farquhair himself, pompous and ordering the workmen about and complaining about the cost and time taken over everything. At dusk, when the builder's van drove off and the dust motes settled, I would come out the chimney and survey the day's changes with dismay. I was feeling very sorry for myself at this point. My hope was that the ghost of Young Hilda would return to haunt *Jonah's Neuk*. I imagined fondly that she would be young again and we would become firm friends and have great laughs together. I had read somewhere that ghosts are lost souls with unfinished business on hand in this time and space we inhabit called life. That is why they are often sorrowful rambling creatures, murdered or murderers in life, spirits cut off before their time, burdened with various secrets, grudges, sadnesses and wrongs, unable to move on. Surely, I conjectured, Young Hilda is a prime contender to haunt this place which she inhabited for more than a century? Her beloved house had meant everything to her until abruptly one icy morning she fell and was taken away to a hospital. And then what had happened next? In my mind's eye I pictured the scene, Doris and Farquhair conning and swizzling and smooth talking a disorientated and helpless bedridden old lady out of her home while telling her soothingly it would be all for the best. Then I pictured them talking to the doctors and nurses in the same reasonable manner and everyone agreeing that it would all be for the best – except Young Hilda. But the ghost of Young Hilda never came, no matter how long I waited up and nor did the ghost of Old Hilda or Belle or any other ghost, come to that.

It was a horrible business and as I cowered in the chimney I could feel the old house groan and writhe around me in its torment as its innards were ripped and wrenched out. Imagine a major operation or root canal treatment without any pain killing drug. Imagine open heart surgery where the heart is torn out and replaced with a cheap plastic version from B&Q. Some houses never survive if the alterations are too drastic – they just hang on like dead trees with no sap of life in them. Others become monsters of themselves – haunted things who bear humans ill will like elm trees. All was noise and choking, throttling dust.

Doors were pulled off, windows punched out, walls burst open so that new pipes and wires inserted. Old carpets were exhumed, tugged up and lugged into the rusty skip. Underneath one carpet lay some of Belle's old lino – she had loved that new fangled invention – cheap and clean and so easy to mop the fish scales and blood away.

The conversion, as Farquhair called it, took longer than he had hoped and cost more, despite his penny pinching, cost cutting and blatant encouragement to the builders to ignore health, safety and building regulations. The last major alterations to the house had probably occurred in the early Victorian period, although there had been an inhabited building on the site long before that – I knew as much because Roller Skate had told me that the last substantial changes had seen off the hoose daemon before me – an unpopular and grumpy chap who left on the black ship before I ever came into being. I always wanted to ask Roller Skate about him to find out more but I never got round to it and I suppose it's too late now. There's always something that goes before you though – has to be. There had been much delight and surprise among the Seahouses daemon fraternity when I had shown up a few years later. It was seen as a good omen for the new house. The house of Belle, Old Hilda and Young Hilda hadn't significantly changed during my time.Then in a week it was transformed.

Although I was unaware of it at the time, from the 1850's onwards marked a period of time in Britain that has in many ways left an indelible mark and is still around us. Much of the infrastructure, architecture and fabric of our world was refashioned from this time and we take it for granted. Belle's house did not possess an indoor water closet – there was an ash pit out the back and an earth toilet. It became very smelly in the summer and it was always a great relief when the dustbin men came round with their horse drawn cart and took the mess away. It was around this time that a link was made between poor sanitation and the terrible water borne and infectious diseases such as cholera, typhoid and dyptheria that killed so many. New sanitation laws came into place. I can remember the rejoicing that took place when the first water closet was installed in the house and the occupants had no longer to go out the back in the freezing winter or use the chamber pot beneath the bed. Yet when the change came I resented it and resisted it. For many years I refused to even go in there. But that is the nature of hoose daemons – to resist change. It is in our DNA despite the fact that it is often a perfectly pointless and self defeating way to be. Now I consider the thousands of children who die in third world countries everyday due to drinking poisoned water and I cannot understand how humans are unable to do something about it. They are seemingly able to send a man to Mars, they can manufacture a computer with a memory large enough to contain the wisdom of every book ever written yet they cannot find a consensus to achieve this one doable thing. Oh foolish man!

To begin with, water was brought to the house, carried by Belle in buckets from the outside well. Water was heated on the fire in the copper for washing clothes and occasionally, bodies. There was a coal cellar out the back to keep a good supply necessary to heat the water as well as the rooms. It was seen as another huge leap forward when first cold running water was installed and then a gas boiler was put in – some time in the late twenties I recall – to provide the luxury of hot running water. The early house was candle lit. I used to love that. Then the gas came and lighting became less precarious and winter nights less mysterious. Initially there was a gas meter beneath the stairs. It was fed coins and was exceptionally greedy. The arrival of electricity finally put paid to the last of the winter ghosts though. Now on a stormy night the rain beats soundlessly and the wind rages in vain against the double glazing. A hurricane may pass over as violent as the Eyemouth storm and I hardly even notice it. I can remember the old sash windows rattling like the bones of a pirate swinging in a gibbet cage. What I forget though is that the old sash windows in their turn were new wonders brought about through the abolition of the glass tax, the advances in technology that provided mass produced materials in standard sizes and the new railways that brought bricks and roof tiles and cement.

Is the lifespan of a house like life itself? It seemed that in my youth all was building and strengthening and improvement toward progress. Then came the middling years. All, more or less, is what it should be, some maintenance needed perhaps, a new coat of paint, the occasional roof tile blown off in a gale that requires replacement, a wobbly slab wanting fixed by the door. And then, all too soon, suddenly the house is found not fit for purpose. Behind the stolid unchanging exterior all is found to be dated and faded, rotting and ill equipped for modern life. This tearing down of supporting beams, these partition walls, that extra bedroom squeezed in, the en suite bathroom – all of which tear my heart itself in pieces – is this perhaps, simply the birth pangs of rebirth? One of young Hilda's favourite poets, Thomas Hardy, would have known the answer. Another of her firm favourites, Robert Louis Stevenson, who once wrote a great nautical yarn, also wrote:

> My house, I say. But hark to the sunny doves
> That make my roof the arena of their loves,
> That gyre about the gable all day long
> And fill the chimneys with their murmurous song:
> Our house, they say, and mine, the cat declares
> And spreads its golden fleece upon the chairs.

CHAPTER EIGHT

The Clear White Light

Lay down my dear brother, lay down and take your rest,
Won't you lay your head upon your savior's chest,
I love you all, but Jesus loves you the best
And we bid you goodnight, goodnight, goodnight.

I would never ride, well, I would never ride
(goodnight, goodnight)
But His rod and His staff, they comfort me
(goodnight, goodnight)
Tell "A" for the ark, that wonderful boat
(goodnight, goodnight)
Tell "B" for the beast at the ending of the wood
(goodnight, goodnight)

You know it ate all the children when they
wouldn't be good,
Walking in Jerusalem just like John
(goodnight, goodnight)
I go walking in the valley of the shadow of death,
And we bid you goodnight, goodnight, goodnight.

A year later and Christmas Eve was bitterly cold. I could not remember it ever being colder. Further inland the snow was lying on the tops of the dark silent hills. Snow seldom came to Seahouses because it lies at sea level, as its name suggests, but a deep frost had set in covering everything with a glittering rime. The pavements, polished by the feet of last minute shoppers were like marble and extremely treacherous for old folk. Trees and buildings and grass and tarmac were covered with ice and frost that glinted like fire. I took a walk along the dunes and stiff marram grasses, gulping down cold raw air that rasped my lungs. There the shallow foamy waves had hardened into fantastic ice sculptures at the point where they had crashed onto the beach. A shrill Baltic wind was screaming in from the East driving and whipping the white horses. The long pale arm that reached out from Longstone seemed particularly ghostly that night. I felt sorry for the poor seabirds – none of whom were to be seen or heard. Were any still alive in this deep freeze? I felt even sorrier for any poor fishermen who were out this night on the tumbling waves. It was a night to be couried up beside a glowing fire with a dram or tucked up in a warm bed with a hot water bottle. By the time I made my way back along the beach the wind had veered and was blowing down from the North bringing slapping sleet down from the Scottish Borders moors and hills. There were a few lights on in the drafty caravan park beside the golf course – hardy souls who had come up for the holiday season and who were now huddled shivering around an inadequate heater. The holiday houses in the terraced street beside *Jonah's Neuk* were all silent and in darkness. The only thing worse than a dilapidated crumbling old slum is a dilapidated crumbling old uninhabited slum. I could remember when these were all family homes and there would be a Christmas tree in every warm lit window bay and excited bairns hanging up stockings before being packed off to bed. Mums would be busy getting the turkey ready for next day while Dads were away for a quick pint of *Exhibition* or buying a last minute present for the wife indoors.There would be an equally excited hoose daemon in each one of these too, whizzing around the tree, enraptured with the fairy lights. I used to love the buzz of anticipation and optimism that crackled around the town in the run up to Christmas Day. It was always a positive time, unlike the New Year which I have always found to be a maudling and backward looking time of the calendar. This year, the Recession and the awful weather which had closed even some of the big motorways had put paid to any festive bonanza for the town's holiday property owners. The town was dead. It was a still night with a clear sky liberally sprinkled with cold blue stars. Wherever I wandered the sad sighing of the churning sea seemed to follow me. I never met a soul. Heading through the streets I saw lights on in the Church of England. A few old folks were attending a watch night service. I sat on the roof for a while listening to the quavering voices singing hopeful carols. Then I headed home, pinching a piece of tinsel off a Christmas tree to give to Nicey for a present. I was feeling sad and lonely and a bit sorry for myself, the last hoose daemon in Seahouses but I was also kind of glad that I was not sharing my house with a family of noisy boorish pests like the Blackberries. That would have been much much worse than being on my own. I curled up in my attic and fell into a deep sleep. I start to dream. I dreamed about a boat – a dark boat. Not a boat but a ship. Not one ship but three. There is a bang. One of the three ships has run aground. Scraped on a rock that sticks out of the sea.

I know every noise made by every nook and cranny of this old house, every squeaky floorboard, rattling window pane, creaking joist and gurgling pipe. That was why I was awake instantly when I heard a different one. A new kind of noise to me. It might have been a solitary late night reveler coming home from a Christmas party outside, it might have been the cat at the dustbins but it was neither. A strange noise that was outside and inside the house at the same time. A bang, a shove, a scrape, some glass breaking followed by hushed whispered voices. *Jonah's Neuk* was being burgled through the back door where the kitchen was. They had got into the narrow passageway at the back.

As I came downstairs to see what the intruders looked like my heart was thumping. This had never happened before. What was I supposed to do? They might desecrate the beloved house of Belle and the two Hildas. What if they set it on fire? I felt weak and dizzy and full of a dreadful panic. Was I dreaming all of this?

There were two of them, a boy and a girl, not much older than bairns, white frightened faces and shivering in the cold of the small hours. They were not dressed for a winter's night at all. They had on cheap flimsy stuff. Thin coats, trainers, jeans and hoodies. No gloves or scarves. They were whispering to each other, big scared eyes trying to penetrate through the darkness of the kitchen. I could not make out what they said. The girl was holding a bag – a holdall with some replica brand name printed it. To put the ill gotten gains in, no doubt. Tough luck children. Tightwad Farquhar Tinkerson had removed anything of the slightest value long before. All they would find here were cheap ornaments, utility Ikea plastic, dogeared Oxfam paperbacks – crime and murder mainly. So what if? The redtop newspapers that blew about the car parks like crumpled cabbages were always full of stories of drugged up kids causing senseless damage for the sake of it. Would they burn *Jonah's Neuk* down? The boy bumped into the edge of the kitchen table. Now he was fumbling for a light switch. The girl hissed at him. I couldn't understand the words. Not local then. Was it Polish? Further East, maybe?

From some far flung God forsaken place. But I understood the tone. "Don't be stupid, you fool! We don't want to be seen." It was like an ice box in that kitchen. No wonder the two of them were chittering like skinned rabbits. The Tinkerson tightwad, knowing there were no paying guests coming, had turned off everything. Electricity, water – not wanting burst pipes and floods or the clean up bills that followed . . .

Then the hallway begins to light up slowly. It fills up with light, illuminates with a radiance like the old monks' bibles. The light permeates through to the back kitchen. It lights up the faces of the night visitors and I see how young and scared they both are. Terrified. They whisper urgently and duck down under the table. I feel the tension crackling in the freezing air. I go through to the hall. There is a big white car, moving very quietly, almost silently. There are four or five hard faced young men inside it, looking, searching, probing. The car stops in the close. They are talking. The headlights are flooding the front of the house. The driver, slightly older, is giving orders, his eyes as cold as Herod's. The four others get out of the car. They are careful with their footfalls. They are carrying knives that glint like the frost. The kind of knives Belle could gut a herring in the blink of an eye with. How I wish old Belle were here now. So fearless and resolute. The men/boys fan out across the street, shining torches into the sightless eyes of the shut up dead holiday homes. Behind me from the kitchen I hear a strange cry. Not a fearful cry. The cat? No – it is a baby's cry. A baby happed in a holdall.

That's what it is – no mistake. The kids have a baby. They are a couple. But outside in the stillness the searchers are coming nearer. It is still and silent enough to hear a baby's cry in the night. Be still and quiet please little baby. Two of the thugs approach the front door – one turns the handle softly. It is locked. Their footsteps scrunge on the gravel outside and I can hear them talking in low conspiratorial voices. They move from doorway to doorway with their torches in the shadows, death angels. One of them is shining his torch directly into the front room. One of them is looking down the side passage that leads to the back of the house. If he goes down there with his pointing inquisitive torch he will see that the back door has been forced wide open. The young couple cowering under the kitchen table will be discovered and taken. No time to lose.

I belt up the chimney and slither out onto the roof. I skitter along the roof ridge and quickly reach next door's chimney stack. I slip down their chimney and gain access to their living room through their fireplace. *Seacrest* – another empty holiday home. But its owner has not switched off the electricity supply. And it has a working burglar alarm and security lights – and I am able to dance in the beam and trigger the lights while my trembling dancing presence vibrates the alarm. Outside the two men leap back into the shadows when the lights come on and the whirling wheepling swallow hiss alarm noise starts up. I want to divert them but also to make them think that this house is occupied – but not by their frightened quarry, who would not draw attention to themselves, but by Yuletide holiday revelers.

Then there is a call – an urgent curt command from their master. Calling in his attack dogs. They return to the car quickly and obediently and get in. It is driven off, this time its driver not caring about the noise of the engine. Rap music begins to beat and throb. The car roars away. The sound fades in the night. I return to the roof. Within a few moments a new light appears. A blue light. this has all happened so fast . . .

A blue light flashing but no siren. The police car pulls up cautiously and comes to rest. The engine and lights are switched off and two officers get out and approach *Seacrest*. The security lights are on still but the alarm soon silences itself. Next door, *Jonah's Neuk* is in darkness. One policeman tries the door of *Seacrest Cottage*. His turn to try the windows and poke his torch beam into the interior. "No sign of a break in," he tells his colleague,"Bloody faulty alarms – probably a cat or a bird. God, I hate seagulls.

Flying bloody rats!" It is the early hours of Christmas morning, the end of a long shift. He wants back to the station for a coffee and a mince pie.

"I'll take a quick look round the back and check anyway," the other policeman says. He disappears down the close that leads to the cramped passageway at the back of the houses. I feel myself growing tense. My heart thrums with anxiety. From the slates on the roof I cannot see down into the passageway but I can hear him rooting around. A wheelie bin is pushed back. A door handle is turned. A window is fumbled at. "No – nothing amiss,it's ok." he calls finally.

"No sign of a big white car either," his mate shouts, "Don't know what that caller thought was going on. Too much Christmas cheer."

"Yeah, you're right there," the other policeman jokes, "drinking the milk left out for Santa. Best be off then – I'll radio the station." There is a crackling in the night air as he gets back into the car and reports back. The engine of the police car starts up.The blue light is not switched on this time. The car purrs off into the dark. The security light of *Seacrest* switches itself off. I slither down to the back door of *Jonah's Neuk*. The forced door has been shut. The broken glass gathered. The young people have had time to clear up. Make everything look normal – in this case normal meaning deserted and uninhabited. The policeman has not noticed anything. Horizontal stinging sleet is blowing in from the East.

Merry Christmas!

So here I am. Still here in *Jonah's Neuk*. Once again there is a babby in the house and that is a blessing indeed and makes me feel happy. The Christmas morning sky is greying to greet a sub zero day. Will there be a sun to see at some point? Mind you, it is warm and cosy as toast in the old house. On my return, I was a busy daemon indeed. It took a lot of effort – more strength than I've used up in years in fact, but somehow or other I managed to move that stiff obdurate switch on the meter board in the little cupboard under the stairs. The power's back on. Hot water is coursing through the singing ringing pipe veins of the house. Hot water is a necessity for heat, hot showers, cups of tea and of course, looking after babbies and their multifarious needs. All on the house, free of charge, courtesy of Mr. Farquhair Tinkerson. We don't want the lights on in case any nosey parkers come along but Joe and Marie have found the candles in the cupboard above the sink – I left the cupboard door open for them. I like candles – reminds me of the old days and the dim yellow oil lamps. Whale meet again. Makes things appear mysterious and magical. I don't really understand their language or their full story but the two of them look like they have been through a rough and highly dangerous time. They're exhausted. You could say stressed out. They're sound asleep right now in the front bedroom, cuddled up like me and Nicey. Beside them, in the ill shapen box that Willie the Scotsman made in the shed with the mermaids carved on it with a nail lies the new babby, all pink and warm and wrapped up in a thick blanket. Nicey and I are doing a bit of baby sitting.

I'm glad now that I didn't set off for *Fiddler's Green* too early – or rather that the dark boat didn't come calling too early. I knew there was something important I had to do here before I moved on. Besides, the blokes will all be fine – they'll be sitting boozing in some bar yonder playing darts and dominoes and cracking jokes until I arrive. I'll wait a bit into January until Joe and Marie think it's time to head off before I leave with Nicey. But for now the big wide world lies out there waiting and biding its time – it's cold eyed and dangerous and angry like a starving wolf. But for now, we're all safe and cosy and living in the moment in our little ark of souls. When they do head off they'll have a nice little nest egg to take with them to help them along the way. A monetary miracle happened last night. A load of tenners and twenties blew down the chimney in a gust of soot. Santa must have broken wind in the chimney. You should have seen the surprise on their faces. Only at Christmas, eh!

The babby is awake. Cooing and gurgling, a contented wee miracle. It has big black eyes that sparkle like the sunlight across rock pools. It can see me quite clearly and hear me too. So I tell it my whole life story here in *Jonah's Neuk* and about all the folk who have lived here. It seems to like the sound of my voice and be quite interested in my tale. I believe it is laughing at me as I sing softly to it:

Come here, ma little Jacky
Now I've smoked me backy
Let's hev a bit o'cracky
Till the boat comes in

Dance ti' thy daddy, sing ti' thy mammy,
Dance ti' thy daddy, ti' thy mammy sing;
Thou shall hev a fishy on a little dishy,
Thou shall hev a fishy when the boat comes in.

Here's thy mother humming,
Like a canny woman;
Yonder comes thy father,
Drunk---he cannot stand.

Dance ti' thy daddy, sing ti' thy mammy,
Dance ti' thy daddy, ti' thy mammy sing;
Thou shall hev a fishy on a little dishy,
Thou shall hev a haddock when the boat comes in.

Our Tommy's always fuddling,
He's so fond of ale,
But he's kind to me,
I hope he'll never fail.

Dance ti' thy daddy, sing ti' thy mammy,
Dance ti' thy daddy, ti' thy mammy sing;
Thou shall hev a fishy on a little dishy,
Thou shall hev a bloater when the boat comes in

I like a drop mysel',
When I can get it sly,
And thou, my bonny bairn,
Will lik't as well as I.

Dance ti' thy daddy, sing ti' thy mammy,
Dance ti' thy daddy, ti' thy mammy sing;
Thou shall hev a fishy on a little dishy,
Thou shall hev a mackerel when the boat comes in.

May we get a drop,
Oft as we stand in need;
And weel may the keel row
That brings the bairns their bread.

Dance ti' thy daddy, sing ti' thy mammy,
Dance ti' thy daddy, ti' thy mammy sing;
Thou shall hev a fishy on a little dishy,
Thou shall hev a salmon when the boat comes in.

Bonus Chapters

Passing Ghosts

Tammy Norrie's Poems

SEALS

A boring brown shoreline of stones
then three whiskered boulders flip
themselves into the sea.

OLD VICTORIAN GENTLEMAN SEAL

In Astrakhan coat
huffs, puffs, shuffles and sneezes,
takes life with a pinch of sea salt.

SEAHOUSES

Serenity and *Glad Tidings*
are home and harboured for the night
beneath the lighthouse Venus.

LONGSTONE

From a haunted window
a million ghosts of candle power
arc over the whale's cold acres.

CORMORANTS

Oily and drenched,
they hold up their wings
like anorexic batsigns.

PUFFINS

Dustin Hoffmans with painted noses
and a lust for sand eels:
like middle aged men with novelty ties.

OTTERS

A fishy diet's what fuels and gyrates them –
living proof of all that's spoken for sea fare:
supple boned as salmon, cannier than silkies.

ROCK POOL

Water and sunlight , aqua and lux
clearer than super HD:
Runey the crab makes a run in the box.

LAND AND SEA

Softly sea licks land
like a cat her kitten:
igneous, unyielding and masculine -
land will not be smitten.

Hard the land thrusts out a fist
into the soft wet sea:
Ten million years from now
she'll have ate him for her tea.

KITES

A lime green kite is hanging high
over a cold porridge beach -
a heartsome soul upholder.

A blown red kite is laid low,
its strings tangled in the grass -
a daemon is brought down.

A still calm day without a gust -
till a gold kite torques the Earth to sky
and makes the rumpled wind go mad.

ANOTHER KITE

A puffed up poke, skittering over a beach,
a cheap thing blowing by,
far out of reach,
thin rustling plastic, high in a heavy sky.

How I loved what it brought,
how it lifted the dead weight of circumstance:
a child's silly thought -
that somehow there's always a chance.

COUNTING

Yan, tan, tether, mether,
Four hoose daemons all together.

Pip, azer, sezar, akker,
Eight hoose daemons making clatter.

What comes next? *Conter, dick,*
Ten hoose daemons scraping sticks.

Yan, tan, tether, mether,
Cold hoose daemons in the weather.

Numbers learned from long gone Picts -
Nae hoose daemons playing tricks.

TREASURE

Smelt the impurities
from the dross of words
to be wrought into a rhyme cage.

One day a saga,
an ingot, a seam,
another a fine fleck of language.

But use all the hoard that comes to hand,
the sun glint among the moon – pale sand.

THREE SHIPS

Body Ship
Keeled with backbone
Straked with ribs
Clinkered with skin

Limbs the rowers
Lungs the sails
Brainhouse the foc'sle
Brain the skipper
Heart the lodestone

Eyes the lookouts
Set high in the mast to scan

BURIAL SHIP

Ship of stone
Coffin of oak
Ballast of grave goods
Cargo of soul

Sailing beyond
The coils of the worm

STAR SHIP

When night's eyes droop
Where blue stars drop
In the candling of day
Dragon prows bow
Dip under the sea.

SONG

Climb into my boatie
I'll take you for a sail
We'll maybe catch a cod,
A mackerel or a whale,
We'll maybe catch a mermaid
Then we will be enthralled,
The chances are more likely
That we will catch the cold.

THE BINARY WORD

God the bard made a metaphor out of nothing
and meanings matrixed and mixed
exponentially.

EXTINCT

Able to fly like a bird in the sea
But not in the air.
When man first set his foot on its rock
The last Great Auk
Became even more rare.

IN THE MOMENT

From the gift of a million moments granted
I have lived in a handful only.
The poet's task is the impossible:
to net the whole shoal,
to halt the encroaching tide of stars,
to lift the bairn moon unwakened from a village puddle.

For I would encode the unencodable,
the sigh of the churning sea
like some crazy white – coated scientist.
But tonight there is barely a ruffle:
My ghostly muse snores oblivious
And my words steep in a muddle.

GHOSTS

Ghosts are always a let down
like reruns on *UK Gold* on cold afternoons
when the wind vibrates the satellite dish.

They replay the tired sad plots of their lives,
self obsessed and never touch the present.
Ghosts are like kippers, forever coming back.

THE DAEMON'S SHANTY

(To be sung in a rousing fashion while swinging a tankard of ale)

Chorus: *And the ocean waves do roll,*
And the stormy winds do blow,
With we jolly hoose daemons aloft on every roof
And the landlubbers lying down below.

Then up stood Bob Cod, the boldest of them all
For a fine brave bloke was he,
I'll catch me Moby Dick and fry him in beer batter
with chips and vinegar and mushy peas.

Then up stood wee Lingy, though we could hardly tell
For he was somewhat challenged vertically,
"Though I be small and humble, I follow old Tom Paine
So let us drink to the end of Royalty!"

Then up stood Roller Skate, he was a learned man,
He'd read up every book in libraries ,
"Ahem -' he cried, "me hearties, I'd give all me dusty tomes
For a cuddle with a mermaid out the sea!"

There was Lamphray, there was Bedey, there was Whitebait, Scampy Finnan,
There was Eilden, Harry Haddock and Crabbee,
A drunken crew of daemons, sailing half seas on the roofs,
Old salty dogs that never set to sea.

Chorus: *And the ocean waves do roll,*
And the stormy winds do blow,
With we jolly hoose daemons aloft on every roof
And the landlubbers lying down below.

A BROTHER SLIPS AWAY

The geese come cackling over in November
Pilgrim souls who fly from here to yonder
One takes the lead as they pass overhead
Marshalling the sprawling arrowhead.

I recognise that voice above -
He was a soul that I once loved,
Now moves on in another guise
Far out of sight I hear his cries.

Into the dark, an elder brother gone,
While all the foolish world goes laughing on.
How it all ends I cannot tell:
I never had the chance to say farewell.

Bonus 2

From Farquhair Tinkerson's Inventory of Contents of *Jonah's Neuk*

Item description:	*Classification:*	*Notes on Profitability:*
Two armchairs plus sofa	yellow	Upholstered with a brocade type of material in green and brown unfortunately moth eaten est. small profit?
Two porcelain chamber pots	red	Handle missing + cracked Handle missing + cracked
Framed picture print "Bubbles"	yellow	Given away with Pear's soap; v. common
Framed picture "His Only Pair"	yellow	Yuck! Victorian sentimental crap mother mending son's only pair of trousers
Framed Picture "Wreck of Forfarshire"	yellow	Melodramatic wet stuff
Lace parlour curtains	red	Filthy
Fish knife – silver	yellow	Could be buffed up
Tea caddy – Cutty Sark	yellow	Collectible – yum yum!
Brown tea pot	red	Junk – get rid
False leg, left	red	Good grief!

Item description:	*Classification:*	*Notes on Profitability:*
Victorian Boiling "Copper"	yellow	Used to wash clothes - profitable
Brass Davey Lamp	yellow	Coal mining tat
Figure of Miner made of coal	yellow	Maggie, Maggie, Maggie!
Small 3 shelve book-case	green	Keep it for the plebs
Box, wooden, carved	red	Useless – primitive
Cassettes & CD's	yellow	Spoken word, mainly Literature; folk music – awful June Tabor not suit-able for guests need some D. Ross
Ships in bottles	yellow/green	Loads of; keep a few for seaside ambience
Bible	red	Well worn – valueless
Fruit dish, glazed	yellow	Pennies only
Candle sticks, brass	yellow	Mad Goth couple next door have made an offer
Sugar tongs	yellow	A & C movement
Doll's House – home made	yellow	Might con some oik
Model ship, Zulu class	yellow	Some sad anorak sea geek will buy
Barometer, broken	yellow	Pubware
Dominoes	red	double four missing
Two china dogs	yellow	One dog has no nose. How does it smell ? Terrible!
Glass balls in fishing net	yellow	Good for drowning cats in

Item description:	*Classification:*	*Notes on Profitability:*
Fig, old fishermen with sou'wester	yellow	Captain Pugwash?
Lobster creel	yellow	Sell to chip shop
Scallop shells	yellow	Ditto
Comp. W. Shake-speare	yellow	2nd hand bookshop
Ency. Britt. Complete	yellow	2nd hand bookshop
Set of Waverley Novels	yellow	2nd hand book shop
Animal Farm 1st ed, Left bk Club	yellow +	Jackpot!
Monogrammed dressing gown	yellow	50's style – ding dong!
Canteen of cutlery	green	Far too good for the old bat – pater's birthday pres
Zimmer	red	She should have used it more
Shortbread tin of old letters	red	Worthless – to be burned

Bonus 3

- From Introduction: Dr. Skate's *Geological And Ornithological History of the Farnes Islands*

The Farne Islands (also referred to less formally as the Farnes) are a group of islands off the coast of Northumberland in North East England. There are between 15 and 20 or more islands depending on the state of the tide. They are scattered about 2.5–7.5 km (1½–4¾ miles) distant from the mainland, divided into two groups, the Inner Group and the Outer Group. The main islands in the Inner Group are Inner Farne, Knoxes Reef and the East and West Wideopens (all joined together on very low tides) and (somewhat separated) the Megstone; the main islands in the Outer Group are Staple Island, the Brownsman, North and South Wamses, Big Harcar and the Longstone. The two groups are separated by Staple Sound. The highest point, on Inner Farne, is 19 metres (62 feet) above mean sea level.

The Farnes are resisant igneous Dolerite outcrops. These would originally have been connected to the mainland and surrounded by areas of less resistant limestone. Through a combination of erosion of the weaker surrounding rock, and sea level rise following the last ice age , the Farnes were left as islands. Because of the way the rock is fissured, Dolerite forms strong columns. This gives the islands their steep, in places vertical cliffs , and the sea around the islands is scattered with stacks up to 20 metres (66 feet) high. Many of the small islands are bare rock, but the larger islands have a layer of clay subsoil and peat soil supporting vegetation. The rock strata slopes slightly upwards to the south, giving the highest cliffs on the south and some beaches to the north.

In the warmer months the Farnes, an important wildlife habitat, are much visited by boat trips from Seahouses. Local boats are licensed to land passengers on Inner Farne, Staple Island and the Longstone; landing on other islands is prohibited to protect the wildlife. At the right time of year many puffins can be seen and these are very popular with visitors; on the Inner Farne, the Arctic terns nest close to the path and will attack visitors who come too close (visitors are strongly advised to wear hats). Some of the islands also support a population of rabbits , which were introduced as a source of meat and have since gone wild. The rabbit and puffin populations use the same burrows at different times, the puffins being strong enough (with a vicious bite) to evict the rabbits from the burrows during the nesting season. The islands also hold a notable colony of about 6,000 grey seals , with several hundred pups born every year in September–November.

Breeding birds on the Farnes (as of 1990) include:

- Shelduck- 2 pairs
- Mallard-17 pairs
- Common Eider – 443 pairs
- Fulmar- 276 pairs
- Cormorant – 135 pairs
- Shag – 965 pairs
- Oystercatcher – 39 pairs
- Herring Gull – 72 pairs in 1989 (not counted in 1990)
- Lesser Black-backed Gull – 52 pairs in 1989 (not counted in 1990)
- Ringed Plover – 4 pairs
- Black-headed Gull – 461 pairs
- Black – legged Kittiwake – 4,241 pairs
- Sandwich Tern – 966 pairs
- Roseate Tern – 0 pairs (endangered species) – Several individuals spotted.
- Common Tern – 88 pairs
- Arctic Tern – 180 pairs
- Guillemot – 49,076 pairs
- Razorbill – 365 pairs
- Puffin – 36,285 pairs
- Barn Swallow – 4 pairs
- Pied wagtail – 5 pairs
- Rock Pipit – 20 pairs

A total of 290 bird species have been recorded on the Farnes, including in the 1760s, an example of the now extinct Great Auk N. B. On 28–29 May 1979, an Aleutian Tern, a rare tern from the Aleutian Islands in the North Pacific Ocean , visited the Farnes. It was the first, and still the only, member of its species ever seen anywhere in Europe. It remains a complete mystery how it arrived here, although there has been local speculation that the bird's arrival was linked with the appearance of a unidentified "dark ship" that was spotted in the Farnes at this time and later vanished, just as mysteriously – however this pilots us away from the well chartered clear waters of fact and scientific knowledge and into the unfathomed murky depths of rumour, hearsay and folklore. No anchorage in a scientific, factual essay can be afforded for such.

Bonus 4

Bob Cod's Fishy Tale

So you'd like a story, would you lads? Well, let me see now. Some folks say this is all made up but I swear by Noah's rubber duck that every bit of it is true. Well, it was a long time ago. I'm not sure how long ago. Certainly not in the last two or three centuries but not in the dark old times of the wild Picts from up north either who used to sacrifice folk, gut them and spill their heart's blood on to the dirt to make their crops sprout up so that they could all feed their faces and get drunk. Maybe it was at the start of the latest system – what do they call it – capitalism? Aye, it was just after the start of money, taxes, burghs and all that rubbish.

There was a merchant lived in Seahouses and he was doing very well for himself. There had been a relaxation of the feudal laws and a middle class had risen up to the fore. This merchant owned a ship or two and he had connections. He had it all tied up. He was trading across the grey North Sea – to the Baltic states and the Flemish and the French. Filling his ships up with the stuff they wanted – like coal and salt and fish – and then he would sell it in one of their ports and buy a load of their stuff that he could sell on here. I don't know what. Fancy things you couldn't get here. Fabrics to brighten up a grey Northumbrian day. Geegaws and whigmaleeries, Willie the Scotsman used to call them. Anyhow, this merchant was doing well and he was making a right packet for himself. He had a daughter. A lovely young girl. The mother had died of plague or something so there were just the two of them and their servants.

The problem with him was that the richer he became the

greedier he got. This is not an uncommon thing I understand, although I have no experience of it myself. There was this other merchant in the town. A rival. An old, scheming, conniving, cold, baldy, scabby, lecherous and lascivious old goat with bad breath and a big nose that was always red and running. He was known as Sniffer because of this. Old Sniffer Black he was called and he answered to that as well. This old goat fancied the merchant's daughter. And, what's more, he had offered the merchant a fortune as a dowry for his daughter's hand in marriage. The merchant probably knew it was all wrong but he couldn't resist the gold. The problem was, of course, that his daughter couldn't thole the sight of this old creep. No matter how much the father put forward a case for it and tried to invent good points for him, she wouldn't even agree to talk to him. The father did his utmost. He bribed her. He bought her gifts. He shouted at her and told her she had to obey her father's wishes. But she was a strong willed girl, and besides, she had a secret sweetheart of her own. A handsome young fellow from the poor side of town. He had the good looks of Sir Lancelot and Troilus put together but not a halfpenny to his name to rub against the shiny arse of his breeks.

One day the father decided he was having no more of it. She would be married within the year and that was the end of it. It was then that it all came out about the secret lover. The father was furious. Partly because the boy was almost a pauper, partly because he saw his plans for a large dowry thwarted, partly because this had been going on under his nose without him knowing about it. Everybody else in Seahouses seemed to. He summoned the young Romeo and tried to scare him off with all kinds of threats. He told him that he had powerful friends in the burgh and that if he ever looked near his daughter again he'd have him chased to France. To his credit, the young lad stood up to him. He was respectful yet he stuck to his guns. He told the merchant that he loved his daughter dearly. She loved him back. They both wished to be together. He had nothing in the way of a fortune at present but he was determined to make his way in the world. When he had achieved this, he would be asking the merchant for permission to marry the daughter. At this, the merchant laughed in his face and spat at him. "You've no chance, son," he sneered, "my daughter's betrothed already, to old Sniffer Black. It's all been agreed upon. What made a an upstart like you believe you were good enough to be my daughter's husband?"

At this, the comely daughter burst into the chamber. She had heard the shouting in her sewing room. "This is my true love," she told her father, "and I'll go to my grave before I ever marry thon cold and ugly old carl Sniffer Black with his runny nose."

So there it was. The merchant was furious. He shook with rage and could hardly speak. Spitting feathers, he was. There was nothing he could say anyway to dissuade them and he couldn't think of a way out of his predicament. He ordered the girl to her room and he had the boyfriend thrown out. "You'll be hearing from me soon, my bonny lad, and it won't be pleasantries," were his parting words

The merchant was true to his word. The young fellow was summonsed to his grand house again the very next day. He was nervous as you can imagine. He supposed he might end up in the castle dungeon at Bamborough Castle or in the town stocks. But this time he didn't get the kind of reception he expected. The merchant invited him to sit down by the fire and had his manservant pour the boy a large brandy. "We need to talk, you and I, man to man," he said, all reasonable like. "I can't say I'm happy about this turn of events. I mean, be reasonable, can you see it from my point of view? I'm a business man and well thought of in this town. I can't have my only daughter marrying a beggar boy."

"Yet you would gladly give her away to that old reprobate," replied the boy grimly.

" I don't suppose there's any chance that you would choose to disappear off the face of the earth for a reasonable financial consideration?" asked the merchant, sly – like. "I'd make it worth your while. There's plenty other girls in other fishing villages you know. . ."

"Not a chance," answered the boy, "don't you know that true love doesn't work that way?"

"Right then, " said the merchant with a sigh, "I'm a fair man so I'll tell you what I'm going to do. I'll have a word with one of my skeilly skippers. He's the captain of *The Morning Star*. There's a crew heading out in a few days. First to Flanders and then on to the Baltic ports. I'll put a word in and you can sail with them. When you come back in a few months, you'll be entitled to your share of the profits like everyone else. It'll not be a fortune, mind you – certainly not enough to keep my daughter in the style that's she's used to – but it'll be a start. When you return, you give your wages to me and I'll look after them for you. Think on it as the start of your dowry. Now, you complete four or five of these Baltic runs and in a year's time I'll give you my blessing. OK? You can have her and old Sniffer Black can go and hang himself. But if not – if you don't fancy the hard work or if you blow it all in some tavern in Danzig – then that's it. The deal's off. Now then, I call that a fair offer – so what do you say?" And he stuck out his right hand.

"I'd say I'll be calling you Dad in a year from now," said the boy and shook the merchant's hand. "But what if it takes me longer than a year to raise the money?"

"Don't worry, as long as you are out there working hard, I'll show good faith."And the next morning the boy was away down to the harbour, first thing, to see the dour faced skipper and to make his cross on the bit of parchment. But not before he'd been to see the love of his life and said farewell for the time being. I'll not go into all that was said, but they did the usual lovers' things and professed undying love to each other. He kissed the tresses of her long dark hair and brushed the tears from her lustrous eyes that sparkled like the rock pools down on the shore when the sun reflects on them in summer. And they exchanged love tokens then. She gave him a ring of pure gold given to her by her father. And he, being a poor man's son, had little to offer her in return but his love. But he gave her his knife, a cheap thing with a ram's horn handle and a rusty blade he used for whittling things. But it had his initials on it.

They set sail on the evening tide and soon the rocks and spires and towers of Seahouses were left behind. They headed south, always keeping the coast to their right in sight. They sailed straight down that East coast, looking out for English pirates all the time. Then, when they got as far as Whitby, with its Abbey of Saint Hilda in view up on the cliffs, they headed out across the North Sea, aiming for the Dutch coastline.

The crew were unfriendly and gruff to begin with and did the boy no favours. It was just as well he was a resourceful lad and quick on the uptake. He learned fast and did his fair share so the crew started to take to him. But not the skipper or his first mate though. There were a lot of brigands and cut-throats on the seas at that time. The crew had to take turns during the night to keep watch. On the third night out from Seahouses it was the boy's turn. In the dark, quiet hour before the sun comes up in the East, the skipper and the mate slipped out of their bunks and crept up on deck. The skipper hit the boy hard on the head with the spar of an oar before he even kent they were standing behind him. You could have heard the crack a mile away. The mate grabbed him before he fell. The boy was out cold. They went through his pockets. There was not much in them except for the gold ring which the skipper took charge of. "I'll be needing this," he said grimly. Then together they took an end of him each and hurled him into the sea. There was a splash then nothing was heard. "What was that?" shouted the cook and the rest of the crew were soon all on deck, all sleepy – eyed and dozy, wondering what the commotion was all about.

"Acht, that damn fool of a boy," said the skipper, "he's gone and tripped up over a hawser and fallen overboard. Headfirst. There's no hope for him down there. He can't even swim and even if he could the cold would do for him in minutes. He'll be at the bottom now with his boots and lungs filled with water and coarse salt." And although the crew were suspicious, the skipper pretended that he was in a foul temper because they were a crewman short. "The rest of you will just have to work all the harder now we're a man down. That bloody idiot! Mind you, you'll all be getting a bigger share." So they believed his story. After all, the boy was inexperienced. It happened. But that night, when the crew were down below deck, fast asleep, he counted out five Scots pounds to the first mate for his part in the foul business, keeping the other twenty-five that the merchant had given him for himself.

It was a further two months before they returned to Seahouses after a highly profitable voyage. The Skipper, as he had been told to in advance, put on his black coat and a sad face and sought out the merchant and his daughter. "I have bad news for you both," he said, "although the voyage itself went well and we made more silver and gold than we had hoped for, the young fellow, your boyfriend, well, he died, I'm afraid. He was never cut out for life at sea. There's many that aren't. He took sick after just two days. He couldn't stop being sick. Then he took a fever and he just died. We gave him a decent burial – at sea. Before he died he gave me this ring. He asked me to return it and to tell you that you are now free of your love vows to him."

"That is indeed a great shame," said the sly merchant, showing the skipper out the door and winking and slipping another gold ring into his palm for his trouble. Then he turned to his daughter. "You will need a time of grieving, of course, and then you must marry old Sniffer Black – as agreed."

It was a quiet still night and Bob Cod had us all entranced. "That's a sad story," remarked Lamphray, breaking the spell.

"Ah, but that's not the end of it – you see, the boy survived." said Bob.

"Never," said the Hoose Daemons, "you're having us on."

"Oh but he did, he was a tough laddie, used to getting by on his wits on the street. He'd had a few sore blows to contend with already in his short life. When the cold sea water hit his face he came to and he realised at once what they had done to him. Like any Seahouses urchin he could swim like a fish. He was used to the cold water from swimming, summer and winter, down by the rocks diving into the harbour. So he kept his head up and he kept himself afloat. Luckily for him, the sea was as calm as a millpond. But he was in the dark, the moon had gone you see, and he had no idea where he was headed or in which direction the land was. Then, after about half an hour, he hit this big soft round thing. It was a float, made from an inflated pig's bladder. Some Flemish fishermen had left it there as a marker, for there is good fishing to be had in that spot. It's shallow there – no more than twenty feet deep. At one time there used to be a land bridge between the continent and us that you could walk over without getting your feet wet. That was before the sea level rose. Anyway, the sea bed's littered with mammoth and deer bones and the mackerel and cod and lobsters like it fine down there. So the boy got a good grip of that float and held on for dear life. Presently, the sun came up, as it does, and not long after that the Flemish fishermen showed up in their fishing boat to pull up their creels and nets. You can imagine the shock they got when they found the boy clinging to their float gasping and eyes bulging like a drowned rat.

They had a discussion among themselves to decide what to do. They knew he couldn't have swum out from the coast., it was too far. They thought he might be some kind of sea creature – like a silkie – trying to steal their catch from their creels for his breakfast. It would be bad luck to bring him on board – best just to leave him there. But all the while the boy was shouting the odds at them and trying to tell them that he couldn't hold on for much longer. They couldn't understand his accent even though the words were little different from their own Flemish. Then he was trying to show them that he had been pushed into the sea with gestures which is a hard thing to do when you are already in the sea and exhausted. And eventually they cottoned on and pulled him out although they still thought he was unlucky and ill starred. So they tied him up to the deckhouse and they kept their eyes on him."

"So he made it back to Seahouses then?" said Lingy.

"Well now, it turned out that he was an unlucky passenger after all because on their way back to Bruges, lo and behold, were they not intercepted by French pirates who hove up beside their fishing boat and clambered aboard just a few miles from dry land. They threatened to cut all their throats if they didn't hand over what money they had – they weren't interested in the fish, you see. But the fishermen were poor and had no money to speak of so they offered the pirates the boy instead. And the pirates took him in lieu as they say and bound him chains. They sold him on as a galley slave to some bigger brigands operating out in the Bay o Biscay. And that was him for years – chained to an oar in the bowels of a stinking rat infested war galley."

"So he never got home then?"I asked.

"Well now – that was only the start of his adventures. If I were to tell you all the stories and legends about him that might or might not be true we'd be here till the morning. But I see that Crabby's needing away to his bed so I'll cut it short. Some say, he escaped from his chains at some point and leapt off the ship and swam to shore. He joined the King of France's Scots' regiment and fought with great honour and distinction, till they had to make him an officer. Others say there was some kind of mutiny that he assisted in, that he rose up through the pirate ranks and eventually skippered the ship himself and made his fortune that way. Either way he made much gold. And always he had the same single thought in his mind – to return to his childhood home to marry the beautiful North East lass he had left behind.

Seven years and a day after he had first sailed from the old harbour he landed back in Seahouses with the morning tide. With the rising sun behind him and the wind in his long golden hair, he strode up from the quay. He was headed to the merchant's fine house for he planned to settle with him first. He was a fine figure of a man in his bright foreign uniform and silver buckled shoon and heads turned as he passed by in the High Street. Who was he? Wasn't that face familiar? But no . . . this handsome rich young officer couldn't be that little bag of beggar bones!

Yet the fine merchant's house wasn't as fine as he remembered it. There were weeds growing at the lintel. The door itself was needing a coat of paint. There was no sign of servants. Nevertheless, he took the heft of his beaten sword and hammered on the thick oak panels. "Open the door merchant – it is your daughter's suitor returned from abroad after seven long years," he roared and thundered in a voice that was used to being obeyed – the whole street could hear him.

When the merchant opened the door he did not recognise who it was at first. "Who are you?' he whispered. Then he did and he almost fainted with fright. Was this a ghost returned to rebuke him? But the young man too was surprised and shaken for the merchant had grown old and grey and shrunken and twisted. "Is it yourself?" the merchant groaned in a voice that rattled like rat's bones in a cellar. "No, it can't be you . . . for you died, at sea, the skipper told me . . ."

"Would that be the same skipper who you paid to do away with me, far out at sea where no one could see what went on, and all so that you could marry off your daughter to old Sniffer Black?"

"No, no, you've got it wrong," wavered the terrified merchant, "I, I did no such thing. The skipper came back and he told me you had died of a fever at sea. He brought back the ring. I don't understand!"

"I don't believe you," said the young man, "and if you have forced my sweetheart to marry that grasping old carl then I will surely cleave you with this sword from the crown of your head down to your belly button. Where is she?" And he thrust the steel blade at the scrawny throat of the old merchant. "Tell me where I can find my true love."

"You want to see her do you?" hissed the merchant balefully, "then see her you shall. She is not here. But neither is she at the house of auld Sniffer Black. For she wouldn't marry him, no matter how hard I tried to force her. She is a stupid, wilful, disobedient girl. So I threw her out on the street and you'll find her in the convent down the road, for the nuns took her in. And since that day this house and all my businesses have been cursed. Not one stroke of good fortune or luck has come my way. Ships have foundered on rocks, sunk in storms. Cargoes have been looted by pirates. My fortune is all but gone. But go to her now – your beautiful lover. Go and see her now."

"If you are lying to me again it will be the worse for you on my return, merchant." said the young man. But the merchant just laughed a bitter laugh and shut the door in his face.

So he went to the convent door and he asked through the metal grill if he might see her. And the Mother Superior assented with a nod, for they were a silent order. And she unlocked the door and led him along a low dark corridor. Eventually they came to a tiny dark stone cell, little more than a recess in the thick convent walls. And she was there, at prayer, hooded. And when she saw him and recognised who he was, she pulled back her novice's hood and held up a candle lamp in that dark place to show him her face or what was left it. For when she had been told that her true love had died at sea and that she must marry old Sniffer, she had taken the knife token to her own lovely face and destroyed her beautiful features, bit by bit, so that no man, not even the leering old Sniffer Black, could ever bear to look at her again with covetous eyes. The servants had found her on the floor in a pool of blood, and they had taken her to the nuns who had tried their best with their needles and thread to repair the damage.

And her lover wept and was filled with pity for her and his heart was overcome with a newer and stronger love. For the spirit of true love is stronger than anything in the universe and is never diminished by the passing of years or the changing of mere earthly appearances (which are no more than shadows that flit beneath the moon). All that he noticed were her two eyes that still sparkled like the sunlight in the summer rock pools.